The Three Investigators
in

The Mystery of the Vanishing Treasure

In the crowded exhibition hall, The Three Investigators talked together eagerly. "I bet," said Jupe, "that collection of jewels is worth—"

Suddenly all the lights in the museum went out. Frightened voices rose in the dark. Then came the sound of breaking glass, and an alarm began to clang.

"The jewels!" Pete gasped. "Somebody's stealing them!"

ALFRED HITCHCOCK

and

The Three Investigators

in

The Mystery
of the
Vanishing Treasure

Text by Robert Arthur

RANDOM HOUSE   NEW YORK

The Mystery of the Vanishing Treasure

Originally published by Random House in 1966
First Random House paperback edition, 1980

Copyright © 1966 by Random House, Inc.
All rights reserved under International and Pan-American
Copyright Conventions. Published in the United States by
Random House, Inc., New York, and simultaneously in Canada
by Random House of Canada Limited, Toronto.

Library of Congress Cataloging in Publication Data
Arthur, Robert.
   Alfred Hitchcock and the three investigators in
The mystery of the vanishing treasure.
   Summary: The three investigators take on two mysteries:
the disappearance of an ancient jeweled Japanese belt from
a museum exhibit and the strange antics of a group of gnomes
around an elderly woman's house.
   [1. Mystery and detective stories] I. Title
II. Title: The mystery of the vanishing treasure.
III. Series: Alfred Hitchcock mystery series ; 5.
[PZ7.A744Ai 1980]   [Fic]   79-3520
ISBN 0-394-84452-1

Also available in Gibraltar Library Binding

Manufactured in the United States of America
1 2 3 4 5 6 7 8 9 0

Contents

The Three Investigators
in

The Mystery of the Vanishing Treasure

DON'T READ THIS!
(Unless you've never met The Three Investigators before)

This volume is another case of my young friends, Jupiter Jones, Pete Crenshaw and Bob Andrews, who call themselves The Three Investigators. In it they become involved in a baffling museum robbery, assist a lady troubled by a bad case of gnomes, find themselves on the way to the Middle East to become slaves, and otherwise engage in adventurous exploits that make my hair stand on end.

If you have read any of their previous cases, of course you know all about them. You know that First Investigator Jupiter Jones is stocky, almost fat; that Pete Crenshaw is tall and muscular; that Bob Andrews is slighter and more studious. You know that Headquarters for their firm is a carefully hidden, mobile home trailer in the super-junkyard called The Jones Salvage Yard, owned by Jupiter's aunt and uncle, with whom he lives.

You know that Headquarters is entered by certain secret entrances and exits known only to the boys, and bearing such code names as Tunnel Two, Easy Three, Green Gate One and Red Gate Rover.

You know they live in Rocky Beach, California, a town on the shores of the Pacific, a few miles from that strange and glamorous place, Hollywood. In fact, you know all you need to know, and therefore you have skipped all this. If it happens that you haven't previously met the boys, let the foregoing words be an introduction to them.

And now, forward! The case begins!

ALFRED HITCHCOCK

Chapter One

To Steal the Rainbow Jewels

"I wonder," said Jupiter Jones, "if we could steal the Rainbow Jewels."

His question took his two companions by surprise. Pete Crenshaw almost dropped a soldering iron, and Bob Andrews did drop the composing stick he was using to set type on their old printing press.

"What did you say?" he demanded, looking in dismay at the spilled type.

"I said I wonder if we could steal the Rainbow Jewels," Jupiter repeated, "if we were thieves, that is."

"Which we are not," said Pete firmly. "Stealing jewels is dangerous. People shoot at you and chase you. Anyway, I believe in that old stuff about honesty being the best policy."

"Agreed," said Jupiter. But he continued to stare thoughtfully at the newspaper he had been reading.

The three boys, who called themselves The Three Investigators, were in Jupiter's secluded workshop section of The Jones Salvage Yard. Here, out of doors but under a six-foot roof that extended from the Salvage Yard's tall fence, they worked on rebuilding junk that came into

11

the yard. The part of the profits they received from Jupiter's Uncle Titus kept them in pocket money and helped them pay for such luxuries as a telephone in their hidden Headquarters.

It had been quiet around the Salvage Yard for the last few days. The Three Investigators had had nothing to investigate, not even a missing pet. So the boys had nothing more on their minds than fixing the small antique radio Pete had found in the yard's latest batch of junk.

At least Bob and Pete didn't. Jupiter preferred to keep his mind, rather than his hands, working. When he didn't have a good problem to think about, there was no telling what he would come up with on his own.

Bob looked up from the type case. "I'll bet you're talking about the jewels in the Peterson Museum," he said, remembering the newspaper story his family had been discussing the night before.

"Peterson Museum?" Pete looked blank. "Where's that?"

"On top of a hill in Hollywood," Bob told him. "A great big old house that used to be owned by Mr. Hiram Peterson, the oil millionaire. He left the house as a museum, open to the public."

"And right now it has on exhibition a special display of fabulous jewels," Jupiter said, "sponsored by the Nagasami Jewelry Company, of Japan. It is touring around the United States as a means of getting publicity for its cultured pearls. Many of the items on exhibit are pearls or made from pearls.

"However, two other items are of special interest. The main attraction is the Rainbow Jewels. It is a group of gems—diamonds, emeralds, rubies, and stones of other colors—so arranged that they shimmer with all the colors of the rainbow. Some are very large, and even one of them would be worth thousands of dollars. Altogether, they are worth millions."

"There's also a belt," Bob chimed in. "Something made out of huge gold links and set with square emeralds. The paper said it weighs fifteen pounds. It once belonged to the ancient emperors of Japan."

"You're crazy, Jupe," Pete said. "No one could steal jewels like those. I bet they're guarded like a bank."

"Slightly better than most banks," Jupiter said. "There are several guards always in the room with the jewels. A closed-circuit television set trained on the Rainbow Jewels is watched at all times from the main office. At night the room is criss crossed by beams of invisible light. If anybody broke a beam, it would set off a loud alarm.

"In addition, the glass in the cases has fine wires set into it, which also work the alarm system. If the glass is broken, the alarm goes off. It has its own special electric system so even if a big storm, for instance, knocked out all power, the alarm would still work."

"Nobody could steal those jewels!" Pete said positively.

"But it does offer a challenge, doesn't it?" Jupiter asked.

"Why is it a challenge?" Bob asked. "We solve crimes, we don't figure out how to commit them."

"But we haven't any to solve right now," Jupiter pointed out. "I was hoping Alfred Hitchcock would write us about some interesting problem. But he hasn't, and an investigator should use his time profitably. If we try to figure out whether or not the Nagasami jewels *could* be stolen, we will be gaining valuable experience for solving future jewel robberies. And we'll be getting the criminal's viewpoint."

"We'll be wasting our time," Pete said. "We'd be a lot better off to go take some more skin-diving and scuba lessons. We still have a lot to learn about handling the diving gear."

"I vote with Pete," Bob declared. "Let's practice our diving. As soon as we're good at it, Dad has promised us a camping trip in lower California, where we can catch live lobsters in the rocks."

"That's two to one, Jupe," Pete pointed out. "You're outvoted."

"The newspaper says," Jupiter answered, as if he hadn't heard them, "that this is Children's Day at the museum. All children under eighteen get in at half price, and all scouts in uniform and their leaders will be admitted free. That means any Boy Scouts, Girl Scouts, Cub Scouts or Brownies."

"We haven't any uniforms," Pete said. "That lets us out."

"But we have earned some extra money from helping Uncle Titus all week," Jupiter reminded him. "Also, I have time off coming to me. It is an ideal opportunity to go over to Hollywood and inspect the Rainbow Jewels in the Peterson Museum. At least we should see what real jewels look like. Someday we may be called upon to recover some."

"I have a feeling," Bob muttered to Pete, "that we're going to be outvoted, one to two."

"Hey, I have an idea!" Pete had suddenly become interested. "I know how a robbery could be worked. Jewels are stones, aren't they? Well, what do you do with stones?"

"Study them under a microscope," Jupiter said.

"Throw them at tin cans," Bob answered.

"Sure," Pete agreed. "But there's something else you can do if they aren't too big. You shoot them from slingshots.

"So that's how the jewels could be stolen. Someone breaks the glass case that holds the Rainbow Jewels. He takes out a slingshot, shoots the gems through the open window, and his accomplices catch them in baskets. Then they make a fast getaway."

"Great!" Bob said.

Jupiter looked thoughtful. Then, slowly, he shook his head.

"There are two weaknesses in the scheme," he said. "First, the accomplices might get away with some of the jewels, but the other thief would certainly be captured by the guards. And," he went on, "there is an even greater weakness. The jewels could not be sent by sling-shot through a window of the museum because——"

He paused, dramatically.

"Well, why?" Pete asked impatiently.

"Yes, why?" Bob chimed in. "It seems like a good idea to me."

"Because," Jupiter told them, "the Peterson Museum doesn't have any windows."

Chapter Two

Excitement at the Museum

An hour later, Bob, Pete and Jupiter arrived at the foot of the little hill on which stood the Peterson Museum. The hill was across the street from Griffith Park, where the boys had often gone on picnics. Several acres of green grass sloped up to an immense stucco house with two wings, each having a domed roof. A winding two-lane road led to the rear of the house, and another came down farther off for an exit.

Cars and station wagons were moving slowly up the entrance drive. The three boys hiked up, keeping well out of the way of traffic. They saw that the parking lot was liberally sprinkled with cars. More were arriving, and more people getting out all the time. Most of the crowd were children, many in scout uniforms.

Dozens of little Cub Scouts, in blue uniforms with gold neckerchiefs, ran around wildly while their Den Mothers tried to calm them down. Troops of Girl Scouts, looking very lady-like, watched them disapprovingly. There were a good many little Brownies, and a few tall Boy Scouts carrying knapsacks, each with a hatchet fastened to his belt.

16

"I want to study the layout of the land," Jupiter told them. "First we'll examine the outside of the museum."

They walked slowly past the rear of the big building. Bob noticed that what Jupe had said about windows was true. There had once been windows in the building, but those on the ground floor and in the domed wings had been filled in. He was staring so hard at the building that he failed to notice a group of small Cub Scouts and their Den Mother. "Oops! Sorry," he said, bumping into one of them and sending him sprawling in the grass. The boy scrambled to his feet, a gold tooth gleaming in a sunny smile, and ran to catch up with his troop.

"Oh oh!" Jupiter said. "Look at that!"

"Look at what?" Pete said, "I don't see anything but the back of the building."

"Look at those wires," Jupiter said. "See? All the electric light wires come from a pole down to that corner and go inside the house in a cable. That could easily be cut."

"Who would want to cut it?" Bob asked.

"Burglers," Jupiter said. "Of course that wouldn't affect the alarm system, which we know is separate. However, it is a weakness."

Now they finished circling the building and approached the front entrance. As they were not in uniform, they each paid twenty-five cents admission.

Inside, a guard directed them to the right. "Follow the arrows, please," he said.

The three went down a hall and found themselves in the right wing, in a big room with a domed ceiling at least three stories high. There was a balcony around one half of the room, and on it was a sign: "Closed."

Many large pictures in ornate carved frames decorated the walls. These were part of the permanent museum exhibition. However, The Three Investigators were not much interested in the pictures. They had come to see the jewels.

"Notice how the pictures are hung," Jupiter said, as they walked slowly past the paintings. "Each one has an invisible support holding it to the wall. In the old days people hung pictures on long wires from moldings near the ceiling. You can still see the wide moldings which they used when this was Mr. Peterson's house."

Pete looked, but he was more interested in the way the tall windows had been blocked out.

"Why'd they get rid of the windows?" he asked. "You're right, nobody could shoot any jewels out of this place, but I can't figure out why they did away with the windows."

"Partly," Jupiter said, "to give more wall surface to hang pictures on. But mostly, I expect, so they could install good air conditioning. Notice how cool it is? Keeping the temperature and moisture always the same helps preserve the valuable pictures."

Slowly they circled the room, then went down a back hallway following a crowd of giggling, pushing young-sters. They came out in the left wing of the museum, where the jewels were on exhibit. Like the other room, it had a balcony running around half of it, but the steps were roped off.

The Rainbow Jewels were in the exact center of the room. A velvet rope prevented anyone from getting close enough to touch the glass case.

"Very good precautions," Jupiter said, as they filed past. "It prevents any thief from smashing the case and running."

They lingered as long as they could, staring at an enormous diamond that flashed blue fire, a glowing emerald, a ruby that burned like a red ember, and a huge shiny pearl. These were the most valuable jewels, but there were others, of all colors of the rainbow, arranged around them and sparkling in the light.

A guard at the corner of the case told them the jewels were valued at two million dollars, and asked them to move on. A giggling bunch of Girl Scouts took their place.

The boys now found themselves in front of a case nearer the wall, just beneath the balcony, where an impressive jeweled belt was displayed. It was more than three feet long and made of great gold links set with enormous, square emeralds. Pearls edged the links, and diamonds and rubies sparkled from the buckle. The whole belt looked as if it would have taken a big man to wear it.

"This is known as the Golden Belt of the Ancient Emperors," a guard standing nearby told them. "It dates back more than one thousand years. The total weight of gold and jewels is nearly fifteen pounds. It is very valuable, but its historic value is much greater than the value of the precious jewels in it. Now please step along so that others may view it."

They went on to look into other cases which held some really amazing things made out of Nagasami pearls—swans, doves, fish, antelope and other creatures —all made of pearls glued together or set into transparent glass frames. The Girl Scouts ooh-ed and aah-ed over them.

The room was quite full now, and Pete, Jupe and Bob stood in an out-of-the-way spot to converse.

"The room is full of guards," Jupiter said. "So obviously no one could plan a daylight theft. It would have to be executed at night. But then the big problem would be how to get in the front door and how to disconnect the alarm wires in the glass cases." He shook his head. "It is my conclusion that the jewels are safe, except from a gang of experienced, well-organized men. That being the case——"

"Ooops, pardon me!" said a man who had bumped into Jupiter. He had been backing up, looking at his watch, and hadn't seen the three boys.

"Oh, hello, Mr. Frank," Jupiter said.

"Do I know you?" the man asked good-naturedly.

"Baby Fatso," Jupe said, using the name by which he had been known when he was a very small boy in a television comedy series. "You appeared with us on a lot of the old shows, remember? You were always the poor fellow who was blamed for the mischief we kids did."

"Baby Fatso! Sure thing!" the man exclaimed. "Only the name doesn't fit any more. I'd like to talk to you, but I can't. It's time for my act."

"Act?" Jupe asked.

"Watch!" Mr. Frank chuckled. "You'll see some fun. There's a guard. I have to get his attention." He raised his voice. "Oh guard, guard!"

The uniformed guard turned, looking hot and irritated.

"Yes, what is it?" he growled.

Mr. Frank pretended to stagger.

"I'm feeling faint," he whispered. "I need water."

Mr. Frank pulled his handkerchief out of his breast pocket to mop his brow. As he did so, something fell on the floor. It was an enormous red stone, like the ruby in the exhibit case.

"Oh, my!" Mr. Frank looked confused and guilty. The guard was instantly suspicious.

"What's this?" he growled. "Where'd you steal that? You've got some questions to answer, buddy!"

He reached out to grab Mr. Frank's shoulder. Mr. Frank started to protest. Instantly the guard put his whistle to his mouth and blew shrilly.

The sound of the whistle seemed to freeze everyone in the room. Every eye turned toward the guard and Mr. Frank. In a moment the other guards had closed in and made a ring around Mr. Frank, who looked more confused and guilty than ever.

"Now, mister——" began the head guard.

He never finished what he was saying. At that instant the museum was plunged into total darkness.

There was a second of silence. Then a dozen voices said excitedly, "Lights, lights! Turn on the lights!"

But the lights didn't come on. The head guard blew his whistle.

"Two guards stand by the center case!" he shouted. "The others, see that no one leaves this room!"

Suddenly the room was in an uproar. Small boys and girls began to cry, mothers called their children, and everyone milled around in the dark.

"Chief!" shouted a guard. "There are kids all around me! I can't get near the center case!"

"Try!" a voice shouted back. "This is a robbery!"

At that moment came the crash of glass, as one of the jewel cases was broken into. Then the clang of an alarm turned the already noisy room into a bedlam of sound.

"The jewels!" Pete gasped into Jupe's ear. "Someone's after them!"

"Naturally." Jupiter sounded as if he were enjoying this. "This is a well-planned jewel robbery. We must get to the front door and see if we can spot the criminals as they try to leave."

"Maybe there's a back entrance!" Bob shouted.

"We'll have to risk that!" Jupe replied. "Follow me!"

Jupe moved like a small tank through the forest of excited children. But as they got to the door they realized that the guards at the outer door were not letting anyone out. A dangerous situation was building up. The hall was already full of frantic people, pushing and shoving to get out. Soon some of the children would fall and be stepped on.

The boys heard a voice shouting, even above the alarm. Then the alarm abruptly shut off, as someone turned the emergency switch that controlled its special electric supply. The voice now sounded very close. It was a man's, and he had a Japanese accent.

"Guards! Outside!" he cried. "Help people out but do not let them leave the area. All must be searched before leaving!"

At this the guards moved aside and a wave of people surged outside. Jupiter, Pete and Bob followed. They saw that the guards were keeping people together on the big front lawn, trying to calm the women and children. A moment later several police cars pulled up, sirens wailing, to take charge.

The crowd at the door was jammed together, as too many people tried to go through at once. "Let's help," said Jupiter, and the boys held back a troop of Girl Scouts until some of the smaller children had filed out. Among the last to emerge was Mr. Frank. He looked flabbergasted as he approached the boys.

"What's going on?" he asked. "There must have been a robbery. But I——"

At that moment a guard pounced on him.

"You're under arrest!" he shouted and hauled Mr. Frank off, protesting.

"I bet he didn't do anything," Jupiter said, "but naturally he will have to answer a lot of questions. I wonder what the thieves stole and how they made their getaway. It doesn't seem likely they came out this way."

Pete looked over the crowd on the lawn. "It's mostly just women and kids," he agreed.

"Of course they'll probably search everybody," Jupiter went on.

At that moment a small Japanese man, who seemed to be in charge, plunged past them into the pitch-black museum, holding a large flashlight.

A minute later he came back, looking stunned.

"They didn't steal the Rainbow Jewels!" he called to the guards, who were still keeping everyone together on the lawn. "They stole the Golden Belt! The case is smashed at the top and the belt is gone! Everyone will have to be searched!"

Jupiter's eyes lit up.

"Golly!" he said. "Why do you suppose they stole that huge old belt when the Rainbow Jewels were so much easier to get away with? It would be difficult for anyone to hide the belt under his clothes. It is too long and lumpy."

"Those Boy Scouts!" Bob pointed to two tall scouts. "They could have smashed the case with their hatchets and put the belt in one of their knapsacks. They're jewel thieves in disguise!"

"That's too obvious," Jupiter said. "They'll be the first ones searched. I'll bet—" he was puffing a little with excitement—"I'll bet they don't find the Golden Belt at all."

As so often happened, Jupiter's prediction proved correct. The Boy Scouts willingly allowed themselves to be searched. Their knapsacks contained only food—they were headed for Griffith Park for a hike and a cookout. They were allowed to go. One by one the others were searched and released. Mr. Frank had been taken away by the police for questioning, and finally only Bob, Pete and Jupiter were left.

The guards dug up flashlights from somewhere and entered the dark museum. The three boys silently followed them.

Inside, the top of the glass case which had held the Golden Belt was shattered. The belt was gone. The jewels in the other cases were intact.

At that moment the small Japanese man saw them and rushed over.

"You boys!" he cried. "What you do here? Why not you go home? Not wanted here!"

"Excuse me, sir." Jupiter whipped out one of the Three Investigators' business cards. "We're investigators. It's true we're rather young, but we might be able to help you in some way."

The man looked puzzled as he read the card. It said:

THE THREE INVESTIGATORS
"We Investigate Anything"
? ? ?

First Investigator . . . . Jupiter Jones
Second Investigator . . . . Peter Crenshaw
Records and Research . . . . Bob Andrews

"The question marks," Jupiter explained, "are our symbol, our trademark. They stand for questions unanswered, riddles unsolved, mysteries unexplained. We attempt——"

"Foolishness! Silly American boys!" the little Japanese man shouted, flinging the card on the floor. "I, Mr. Saito Togati, in charge of security for the Nagasami Jewelry Company, have allowed the Golden Belt of the Ancient Emperors to be stolen. I am disgraced. And three foolish boys wish to add to my troubles by intruding themselves in my way. Go! This is work for men, not for children."

Well, that seemed to be that, as far as Pete and Bob could see.

They turned and trudged out. After a moment, Jupiter Jones followed them, leaving the small white business card lying on the dark floor.

This was one case they weren't going to get to work on.

Chapter Three

A Call from Alfred Hitchcock

The newspapers next morning were full of the strange riddle of the vanishing Golden Belt. Bob, as official keeper of records, clipped stories about the case and pasted them in the firm's scrapbook. While this wasn't actually one of their cases, Jupiter was taking an intense interest in it, reading every word that was printed.

The newspapers told them some facts they already knew, and a few they didn't. The lights in the Peterson Museum had been blacked out by a man wearing mechanic's coveralls. He had been observed strolling toward the back of the museum carrying a heavy wirecutter.

A few minutes later he was seen driving off in a black panel truck. No one thought anything of it at the time but shortly after that the alarm sounded inside and the excitement began. It was obvious he had been working with the gang of thieves inside, on a carefully timed schedule. In the darkness he had created, his accomplices had promptly set to work.

The great riddle, however, was who had been the gang inside? No one had slipped out the back entrance, for

26

the papers said it had been sealed immediately after the alarm sounded, and a guard posted outside. No one had gone out any windows for there were no windows to go out. Everyone had gone out through the front door, and everyone had been searched.

The paper said that Mr. Edmund Frank, an actor, had been questioned and released.

"I wonder what Mr. Frank's story was?" Jupiter murmured, pinching his lower lip. "He pretended to lose a jewel the guard thought he had stolen. Obviously it was just a joke of some kind, perhaps for publicity, and the jewel was just glass."

Jupiter frowned in concentration. "This was certainly the work of a professional gang, working to split-second plans," he said. "That much we can tell from the way the crime was executed. But I confess, I am in the dark as to who they were, where they went, and how they got the Golden Belt out."

"Maybe it was the guards!" Bob exclaimed. "Maybe they got their jobs at the museum just to do this robbery."

Pete and Jupiter looked at him with respect.

"That's not a bad idea, Bob," Pete said. "But I have one too. Maybe the criminals hid in the museum and didn't come out until after everyone else had gone."

"No." Jupiter shook his head. "The papers say the museum was searched thoroughly and no one was found who shouldn't have been there."

"Those old houses sometimes have secret rooms," Pete said. "Remember the secret room we saw in the Green mansion." He was referring to their adventure, *The*

Mystery of the Green Ghost.

"No," Bob butted in. "It was the guards. It just had to be."

Jupiter sat silent, thinking.

"There seems to be no reason for stealing the belt in the first place," he said. "It would be hard to hide, hard to sell, and worth much less than the Rainbow Jewels. Why didn't the thieves take the Rainbow Jewels? Those could have been put right in their pockets, and later sold with no trouble. I bet if we knew the answer to that question we'd be able to solve the robbery."

Jupiter leaned back in a rebuilt swivel chair in their tiny office in Headquarters. He was obviously thinking hard. They could almost hear his brain spinning around.

"Let us add up what we do know," Jupiter said. "First, the lights went out. An accomplice outside attended to that. The guards were hampered by frightened women and children. We can take it for granted that the gang picked Children's Day at the museum on purpose, just because they figured that would happen."

"Right," Pete said.

"Then, as the guards were surrounding the Rainbow Jewels, someone smashed in the top of the case holding the Golden Belt and lifted out the belt. It would take a tall man to do that."

"Some of the guards were tall," Bob reminded him.

"True," Jupiter agreed. "Well, when the alarm went off, everyone ran for the door. There was a big crush. When everyone finally got outside, they were searched by Mr. Togati, that Japanese detective in charge of security, and the guards. Then we were all allowed to go home."

"We were *told* to go home!" Pete said indignantly. "And after you offered to help them solve the case, too."

Jupiter looked a trifled miffed, but he only said, "Undoubtedly they thought we were too youthful to be of much help. Too bad Alfred Hitchcock isn't a director of the museum. I'm sure he could get us an opportunity to solve the case."

"I'm not sure we want one," Pete argued. "So far we're as much at sea as the police."

"There is one very suspicious circumstance," Jupiter said solemnly. "Mr. Frank may know more than he was telling."

"Mr. Frank!" Bob and Pete stared at him. "What do you mean?"

"Remember what happened?" Jupiter leaned forward and lowered his voice. "Mr. Frank told us he was going to do his act. Then he pulled out his handkerchief and dropped a piece of fake jewelry on the floor. That attracted the attention of the nearest guard. He blew his whistle. Then what happened?"

"What happened?" Bob repeated. "Why, everyone in the room looked his way. And the guards all surrounded him."

"Exactly!" Jupiter's manner was triumphant. "It was a diversion. I deduce that under cover of that diversion, the actual criminals did something no one noticed."

"Something such as what?" Pete asked.

"I don't know," Jupiter confessed. "Just the same, the timing was perfect. Mr. Frank dropped the imitation jewel. A guard blew a whistle. The other guards rushed over. A second or two later all the lights went out. In those two seconds the gang was executing some important maneuver."

Bob looked thoughtful. "Jupe, I think you have something there," he said. "But what? Nobody knows still who the gang was or how they got the Golden Belt out of there. So we're no further along than we were."

They were all silent, pondering this.

At that moment the telephone rang.

After the third ring Jupiter reached for it, switching on the little radio loudspeaker, which enabled them all to hear what was said.

"Jupiter Jones?" asked a woman's voice. "Alfred Hitchcock calling."

"Maybe he has a case for us!" Bob yelled. Since Mr. Hitchcock, the famous motion picture director, had become interested in The Three Investigators, he had steered them to several exciting cases.

"Hello, young Jones!" It was Mr. Hitchcock speaking. "Are you busy on a case just now?"

"No, sir!" Jupiter said. "That is, we offered to help the Peterson Museum solve the Golden Belt robbery, but they said we were too young."

Mr. Hitchcock chuckled.

"They should have let you try," he said. "Judging by the papers, you couldn't do any worse than the police. However, I'm glad you are not busy. You may be able to help an old writer friend of mine."

"We'd be glad to try, Mr. Hitchcock," Jupiter said. "What is your friend's trouble?"

Mr. Hitchcock paused, as if trying to think of the

right words.

"I'm not quite sure, my lad," he said. "But on the telephone she told me she is being bothered by gnomes."

"*Gnomes*, sir?" Jupiter's tone was baffled. Pete and Bob, listening, were equally perplexed.

"That's what she said, my boy. Gnomes. Little people, relatives to dwarfs and elves, who wear leather clothes and live underground and dig for treasure."

"Yes, sir," Jupiter answered. "I mean we know what gnomes are—if there actually are any, that is. They're supposed to be mythological and imaginary."

"Well, my friend says they're real. They sneak into her house at night and change all her pictures and books around. They have her very worried, and she wants someone to help her chase them away. She mentioned them to the local policeman and he gave her such a funny look that she refuses to say anything more to anyone she can't trust."

There was a brief silence.

"So what do you say, my boy? Can you help her out?"

"We'll certainly try, sir!" Jupiter said excitedly. "Just give me her name and address."

He wrote down the information Mr. Hitchcock gave him, promised they would report all progress as soon as possible, and hung up. He looked at Bob and Pete triumphantly.

"Well, maybe we haven't got the Golden Belt case," he said. "But I'll bet we're the only investigators who've ever been called upon to solve a case of gnomes!"

Chapter Four

Something at the Window

Mr. Hitchcock's friend, who was named Miss Agatha Agawam, lived quite a distance away in downtown Los Angeles. Jupiter had to get permission from his Aunt Mathilda for Hans, one of the two Bavarian yard helpers, to drive them down in the small salvage-yard truck.

Jupiter's aunt made no objection, for the boys had worked hard around the yard lately. She fed them all—they all ate wherever they happened to be when mealtime came—and as they ate, they discussed the museum robbery some more.

Jupiter urged them to try to think of any suspicious things they might have seen.

"I saw a Girl Scout leader wearing a big bunch of hair that looked like a wig," Pete offered. "Maybe she was hiding the belt under the wig."

Jupiter groaned. Then Bob said:

"I saw an old man walking with a cane. Maybe he had the belt hidden inside a hollow cane."

"You two aren't being very helpful," Jupiter complained. "Wigs and canes! Those would have been good hiding places for the Rainbow Jewels, but not for the belt. It is too big and heavy. Think of something else."

"I can't think of anything," Pete told him. "I'm all thought out."

"So am I," Bob said. "The riddle of the Golden Belt is too tough for me. Let's talk about our new case. I looked gnomes up in the encyclopedia and——"

"Tell us as we drive," Jupiter interrupted. "I see Hans waiting in the truck."

They hurried out and piled into the front seat with Hans. Jupiter gave him the address, in a commercial district of Los Angeles some miles away, and they set out.

"Now tell us what you learned about gnomes, Bob," Jupiter suggested.

"A gnome," Bob said, "is one of a race of little creatures supposed to inhabit the interior of the earth and guard its treasures.

"The dictionary also says that gnome can be used to mean a dwarf or a goblin," Bob went on. "They're all little people who live underground. Except that goblins are uglier and nastier, and dwarfs are skilled blacksmiths who work precious metals into beautiful jewelry for the gnome queens and princesses."

"And they only live in fairy tales," Pete put in. "They aren't real. They're imaginary. They're miss—mith—"

"Mythological," Jupiter said. "Legendary. Creatures of fable."

"Just exactly the words I was going to use," Pete said, with a certain sarcasm. "So what are mythological, imaginary, unreal, and impossible gnomes doing around Miss Agawam's house?"

"That is what we are going to try to find out," Jupiter

told him.

"But nobody believes in gnomes anymore," Pete repeated.

Now Hans spoke up. "You are wrong, Pete," he said. "In the Black Forest of Bavaria there happen to be many gnomes. Also trolls and goblins. Nobody sees them, but everybody knows about them. Very spooky place, the Black Forest."

"See?" Jupiter said. "Hans believes in gnomes. So does Miss Agawam."

"Well, this isn't the Black Forest," Pete answered. "This is Los Angeles, California, U.S.A. What I want to know is why gnomes are fooling around here, just supposing there might possibly be any gnomes."

"Maybe they're digging for gold," Bob said, with a grin. "Gold was discovered in California in 1849. Maybe they've just heard about it and have come here to find some. After all, they are the guardians of underground treasure."

"Whether there are gnomes or not, something mysterious is going on. Very soon we will have more facts to work with," said Jupiter. "I believe we are almost there."

They had reached a very old and rundown section of Los Angeles.

Hans slowed the truck, searching for the street number. They stopped in front of a big boarded-up building. From the outside it looked rather like an Arabian castle, with steeples and domes and lots of gold paint, most of which had tarnished and was peeling away. A faded sign said it was the Moorish Theater, and a newer one said that soon a 12-story office building would be built on that site.

Next they passed a high hedge, behind which they could barely see a dark, narrow building. Then they came to a bank, one of the old-fashioned type made out of cut stone, but with a new front that made it seem more modern.

In the next block, they could see a supermarket, then a line of rather shabby stores. It was obviously a business district.

"We've passed it," Jupiter said, reading the street number chiseled into the stone front of the bank.

"I'll bet it was behind that hedge," Bob spoke up. "That's the only building that could be a private residence."

"Back up and park, Hans," Jupiter directed.

Hans obligingly backed up a few feet. They were now opposite the hedge, which was six feet high and shaggy. Behind the hedge they could glimpse an old house which seemed to be hiding from the busy world outside.

It was Pete who spotted a small sign on a white wooden gate that led through the hedge.

"*A. Agawam,*" he read. "This is the place, all right. But why anyone would want to live here beats me. I'll bet it's dark and spooky at night."

The boys piled out, and Jupiter led the way to the gate in the hedge. It was locked. An old, yellowing card under glass was fixed to the gate. In spidery handwriting it said: "Please ring bell. Gnomes, elves and dwarfs, whistle."

"Gnomes, elves and dwarfs, whistle!" Pete exclaimed. "Golly, Jupe, will you please tell me what that means?"

Jupiter Jones wrinkled his brow. "Well, it sounds as if Miss Agawam really believes in these fairy-tale creatures. We're not gnomes, elves or dwarfs. Still, we may as well start finding out what this is all about. Pete, you're a good whistler. Whistle."

Pete looked puzzled. "Why do we have to do everything the hard way?" he grunted. But he puckered up his lips and whistled like a mocking bird.

They waited. Then they all jumped as a voice spoke from the bushes.

"Yes, who is it, please?"

Jupiter understood at once. Hidden in the bushes was a little loudspeaker. Through it the occupant of the house could speak to anyone at the gate before letting him in. Such devices were common in apartment houses, and he had heard of their being used on large estates.

Peering into the bushes, he could see a little bird house. Undoubtedly it held the speaker, and protected it from the weather.

"Good afternoon, Miss Agawam," he said politely to the bird house. "We're The Three Investigators. Mr. Hitchcock asked us to call to discuss your problem with you."

"Oh, of course. I'll unlock the gate." The voice was sweet and light, rather like a bird's.

A loud buzzing sounded, as the locking mechanism of the gate was worked by a button inside the house. The gate opened and they stepped inside.

For a moment they paused. It was almost as if they had left the city behind them. The tall hedge, higher than their heads, hid the street. On one side the blank brick wall of the old, abandoned theater rose several stories high. On the other side was the granite side of the bank. The two buildings boxed the old house in completely. The house itself was three stories tall and very narrow, its redwood boards peeling from long exposure to the California sun. A small front porch held several boxes of flowers, the only touch of brightness in the yard.

They all had the same thought at the same time. It was like an old house in a story book. More like a witch's house than anything else.

But Miss Agatha Agawam, who opened the door for them as they climbed up on the porch, was no witch. She was tall and thin with dancing eyes, white hair and a sweet voice.

"Come in, boys," she said. "It was very good of you to come. Let me show you to my study."

She led them down a long hall to a large room, full of overflowing bookcases. The walls were crowded with paintings and photographs of children.

"Now, boys," Miss Agawam said, indicating three chairs, "please sit down and let me tell you why I called my old friend Alfred Hitchcock. I've been bothered for several days by gnomes. I mentioned it to the local policeman a few days ago and he gave me such a peculiar look that I—well, I'm just not going to say anything about gnomes to the police again!"

She paused. And just then Bob let out an unexpected yell.

While settling himself in an armchair, he had happened to look toward a window. There, gazing in at them, was a small creature—it certainly didn't look human—wearing a peaked cap. It had a dirty white beard, carried a tiny pickaxe over its shoulder, and was scowling ferociously.

Chapter Five

A Story about Gnomes

"A gnome!" Bob shouted. "Spying on us!"

But before the others could turn around, the little man had vanished.

"He's gone!" Bob cried, leaping up. "But maybe he's in the yard."

He rushed to the window, followed by Pete and Jupe. The window was in a dark recess between two bookcases. He tried to raise it and found his hand touching smooth, unbroken glass. Bewildered, Bob blinked.

"It's a mirror," Jupe said. "You saw something in a mirror, Bob."

Bob turned around, puzzled. Miss Agawam was rising. She pointed in the opposite direction.

"The window is over there," she said. "It does reflect in the mirror, of course. I like that because it makes the room seem larger."

The boys ran toward the open window on the opposite side of the room. Jupe leaned out and peered into the yard.

"Nobody in sight," he said.

Pete joined him. "The yard's totally empty," he reported. "Are you sure you saw something, Bob?"

Baffled, Bob studied the hard ground under the window, the empty yard, the high brick wall of the abandoned movie theater. Nothing was stirring. Certainly there was no little bearded gnome in sight.

"Maybe he ducked around the side of the house," he said. "Because I'm positive I saw him. We ought to search the yard. With the gate locked he can't get out."

"I'm afraid you won't find him, if it was a gnome," Miss Agawam said. "After all, they have magical powers."

"I think we should search," Jupiter told her. "Is there a rear entrance?"

Miss Agawam led them down the hall to a door that opened onto a small back porch. The three boys ran out into the yard.

"Pete, you go left!" Jupe shouted. "Bob and I will go right."

There wasn't much to search. The yard held a few straggly bushes. At the rear was a high board fence, behind which was an alley. There were no holes in the fence, and only one rear gate, which was locked. An iron emergency-exit door was set into the side of the old Moorish Theater at one side of the yard. But the door proved to be solidly locked, and very rusty, as if it had not been opened in many years.

"He didn't go through there," Bob said.

Bob and Jupiter peered into the bushes, then studied the cellar windows of the house. They were all locked, and very dirty. Next they moved to the front hedge. There were no breaks in the hedge. No place a small, bearded figure could have scooted out of the yard.

The strange little creature Bob had seen had evaporated, as far as they could tell, into thin air.

Pete joined them. He had found exactly what they had found—nothing.

"Let's look for footprints," Jupiter said. "Under the window."

They trooped around to the side of the house where the study was. Beneath the window the ground was packed hard and dry—much too hard to show marks of any kind.

"No footprints," Jupiter said, disappointed. "However, another mystery."

"What mystery?" asked Bob.

Jupiter stooped and picked up something. "Look at this. A little blob of fresh earth that might have fallen from someone's shoe."

"Or out of one of Miss Agawam's flower boxes!" Bob retorted.

"Perhaps," Jupiter answered. "However, look up at the window. The bottom of it is above our heads. You say you saw a very small figure at the window, Bob?"

"A gnome about three feet tall," Bob answered. "He wore a peaked cap and a long dirty beard and carried a little pickaxe. I saw him from the waist up. He was looking at us and scowling as if he was very angry."

"How," Jupiter asked, "could a gnome three feet tall stand out here and look in a window at least six feet above the ground?"

The question stumped them, until Pete spoke up.

"A ladder, of course. He was standing on a ladder."

"A folding, collapsible ladder?" Jupe asked with rich

sarcasm. "That he put in his pocket before he scooted into a hole in the fourth dimension?"

Pete scratched his head. Bob frowned.

"Gnomes can work magic," Bob said finally. "It must have been some kind of magic."

"Possibly you didn't really see anything, Bob," Jupiter suggested. "You do have a very strong imagination."

"I saw it!" Bob said hotly. "I could even see his eyes! They were fiery red."

"A gnome with fiery red eyes." Pete groaned. "Oh oh! Couldn't you change your mind and say you imagined it, Bob?"

Bob began to feel doubtful. After all, he had only had that one quick look.

"Well, I don't know," he said. "I think I saw it but I suppose you're right. I was thinking of the picture of a gnome I saw in the encyclopedia and—well, probably I did imagine it."

"Well," Jupiter said, "if you imagined it, we certainly can't find it. And if you really saw it, whatever you saw, it must be able to make itself invisible, for it certainly isn't in the yard."

"And there's no way out of the yard," Pete added.

"We'd better go back in and find out what Miss Agawam has to tell us," Jupiter suggested.

They went back up the front steps. Miss Agawam opened the door for them.

"You didn't find him, did you?" she asked.

"No," Bob told her. "He just vanished. There was no place for him to go but he disappeared."

"I was afraid of that," Miss Agawam said. "That's

how gnomes are. It's very rare, though, to see one in the daytime. Well, let us have some tea and then I'll tell you what has been happening.

"I am sure you boys are going to be able to help me with this strange mystery," she said, pouring from a china teapot. "Mr. Hitchcock said you have solved some very unusual cases."

"Well, we have had some pretty interesting ones," Pete agreed, accepting a cup of tea to which he added a lot of sugar and cream. "Jupe has done most of the solving, though, hasn't he, Bob?"

"About eighty percent of it," Bob agreed. "Though I guess Pete and I helped some, didn't we Jupe? . . . Jupe!"

Jupiter, who had been looking sideways at a newspaper lying on a nearby couch, jumped slightly.

"What?" he asked, and when Bob repeated the question, he said to Miss Agawam, "We work together. I couldn't have done anything without Pete and Bob helping."

"I noticed you were reading the headline about that strange affair at the museum yesterday," Miss Agawam said, offering cookies, of which Jupiter took several. "My, the world is full of mysteries, isn't it?"

Jupiter took time to swallow a cookie. Then he said, "We were actually at the museum when the Golden Belt was stolen, and we are totally baffled by that particular case. We offered to help, but—well, the man in charge thought we were too young."

"He told us to go home!" Pete said indignantly.

"I'm sure he made a mistake," Miss Agawam said.

"But to be very selfish about it, I'm glad you aren't busy on something else. But before we start to talk about my problem, let's enjoy our tea. I never believe in talking about something serious while one is eating."

She poured more tea for them and passed around the cookies. Bob and Pete would have preferred a soft drink, but the tea wasn't bad with plenty of cream and sugar, and the cookies were delicious.

"Oh, my, this reminds me of the old days," Miss Agawam said happily as they ate. "Why, not a week passed that I didn't have a tea party for my very own gnomes and elves and dwarfs."

Bob choked slightly on a cookie. Then Jupiter spoke up.

"Do you mean that you invited the neighborhood children in for tea?" he asked. "And called them your gnomes and dwarfs and elves?"

"Why, of course!" Miss Agawam beamed at him. "You are clever to guess. I'm sure I don't know how you did it."

"Deduction," Jupiter said. He pointed to the photographs on the walls. "You have many pictures on your walls of children dressed in clothes such as were worn a good many years ago. Most of them are signed, 'With love to Miss Agatha,' or something like that.

"Also, you have a whole shelf of books right beside the door which you wrote yourself—Mr. Hitchcock said you were a writer. I noticed several of the titles, such as *The Gnomes' Happy Holiday* and *Seven Little Gnomes*. I deduce therefore that you used to write about such imaginary creatures, and that you probably called your young friends gnomes and dwarfs and elves for fun."

Pete and Bob looked at Jupiter open-mouthed. They had seen the pictures and books but hadn't paid any attention to them.

"Why, you have it exactly right!" Miss Agawam clapped her hands in delight. "Except for one thing. You said gnomes are imaginary creatures. They aren't. They're real. I'm sure of it.

"You see, when I was small my father was well-to-do, and I had a governess from Bavaria. She knew all the wonderful stories about gnomes and the other little people who live in the Black Forest. Later, when I began to write stories, I wrote about the things she had told me. She gave me a big book she had brought with her. It's in German, but you can understand the pictures."

She stood up to get a book off the shelf, a big old book bound in leather.

"This book was printed in Germany about a hundred years ago," Miss Agawam said, turning the stiff pages as the boys crowded around. "It was written by a man who lived for months in the Black Forest. He made drawings of gnomes and dwarfs and elves to illustrate the book. Look at this drawing."

She turned to a full-page picture of a rather terrifying little man in a peaked leather hat. He had large hairy ears, hands and feet, and carried a short pickaxe in his hand. His eyes had a fierce, glaring expression.

"That's like the one I saw peeking in the window—I think!" Bob said.

"The writer calls this 'The Wicked Gnome King,' " Miss Agawam told him. "Some gnomes are wicked and mischievous, but others aren't. The wicked ones, this writer says, have fiery red eyes."

"Ulp!" Bob choked, remembering the glimpse of red eyes he had seen. Well, anyway, thought he had seen.

Miss Agawam turned some more pages, and showed them pictures of ordinary gnomes, who were dressed the same but didn't look quite as mean as the wicked gnome king.

"These pictures look exactly like the gnomes I've been seeing," she said, closing the book. "So that's how I know they are gnomes, and are real. In a moment I'll tell you just what happened. But first let me tell you about the old days when I was a well-known writer of books about the Little People."

She sighed. It was obvious she remembered the old days with great pleasure.

"After my father and mother died, my stories became very popular and I made a good deal of money from them. Of course it was a long time ago—many years before any of you were born—but children often came to visit me and have me sign copies of my books for them. I like children very much and all the children in this neighborhood were my friends.

"Then, the whole neighborhood changed. All the old houses and nice trees were torn down, and shops went up instead. All my old friends, the children, grew up and moved away. Many people wanted me to sell, and move away too, but I wouldn't. I had always lived here and, no matter how things changed, I intended to keep on living here. You can understand my not wanting to leave my old home, can't you?" she asked.

They nodded.

"Things kept changing," Miss Agawam sighed. "A few years ago even the motion picture theater next door had to close. There were so few people living around here to visit it. I put up a card telling my gnomes and elves and dwarfs to whistle to be let in, just for old time's sake. And do you know—once in a while one does come back to visit me. But my goodness! They're grown up now. They're grown up with children of their own, and even grandchildren! That tells you how long ago it was."

She paused. They could easily understand how it had all happened.

"Perhaps I should move now," Miss Agawam said at last. "Mr. Jordan, who is going to tear down the theater next door and build an office building, wants me to sell to him so he can make his building bigger. But goodness —I was born here and I am determined to stay here, no matter how many office buildings they build around me!"

She looked very spunky and determined. The boys could well imagine her defying anybody to make her sell her house.

Miss Agawam poured herself a last cup of tea.

"Well, now I've talked about the past enough. It's time to come up to date. After all these years of writing about gnomes, I didn't really expect to see any. But I did. A few nights ago."

"Please tell us about it," Jupiter requested. "Bob, take notes."

Bob whipped out his notebook. He had taken typing and shorthand in school and was very good at both. Eventually he planned to be a newspaperman like his father.

"I usually sleep very well," Miss Agawam said, "but several nights ago I woke up about midnight and heard an odd sound. It was the sound of someone using a pickaxe to dig, deep underground!"

"A pickaxe? At midnight?" Jupiter asked.

"Exactly. At first I was sure I was mistaken. No one digs anything at midnight. No one except——"

"Gnomes!" Pete finished her sentence.

"Yes, gnomes," Miss Agawam said. "I got up and went to my window. Out in the yard I saw four tiny figures playing. Little men, dressed in what looked like leather clothes, were playing leapfrog and doing somersaults in my yard. I couldn't see them too clearly, of course. I opened the window and called to them. And they vanished!"

She looked at the boys, frowning.

"I was sure it was no dream, and the next day I told the patrolman who covers this neighborhood, Officer Horowitz. You should have seen the look he gave me. Well!"

Her blue eyes flashed indignantly.

"He told me to take care of myself. And he asked if I was going away on vacation soon. I swore then and there I certainly wouldn't say another word about gnomes to the police!"

After a moment, Miss Agawam laughed.

"My pride was hurt," she said. "Anyway, the next two nights I woke up and heard them again. But I pretended to myself I just imagined it and I said nothing to anyone. The third night, however, I knew they were really there.

"I went to the telephone and phoned my nephew Roger. He lives in an apartment a few miles away—he's a bachelor and my only relative. I begged him to come right over, and he agreed to get dressed and start at once.

"While I waited for him, I decided to look into the cellar where the noise seemed to come from. I crept down the cellar stairs without making a sound or turning on the lights. As I went, the noise got louder. Then I turned on my flashlight and—do you know what I saw?"

All of the boys were keyed up by Miss Agawam's story. Bob burst out, "What?"

Miss Agawam lowered her voice. She looked at each of them in turn. Then she said:

"Nothing. I didn't see anything at all."

Bob let out his breath in disappointment. He'd been so sure Miss Agawam must have seen—well, he couldn't guess what. But something.

"No," Miss Agawam told them, "I didn't see anything. I turned to go back upstairs and wait for Roger. And then I saw something.

"I saw a little figure only three or four feet tall. He wore a peaked cap, leather coat and trousers and pointed leather shoes. He had a dirty white beard, and in one hand he carried a little pickaxe. In the other he held a candle. By the light of the candle I could see his eyes glaring at me. They were fiery red eyes!"

"Just like the one I saw peeking in the window!" Bob exclaimed.

"Oh, it was a gnome all right," Miss Agawam agreed.

Jupiter was pinching his lower lip and looking puzzled. "What happened then?" he asked.

Miss Agawam's hand trembled a little as she drank her tea. "The gnome snarled at me. He raised his pickaxe in a threatening way. Then he blew out the candle, and I heard the door at the top of the steps slam. When I got up courage enough to climb the stairs and try the door, it was locked.

"I was trapped in the cellar!"

They stared at her, their eyes round. Suddenly, at the far side of the room, there was a tremendous crash. All of them, even Miss Agawam, jumped.

Chapter Six

Strange Talk Overheard

"Gracious!" Miss Agawam gasped. "What was that?" Then she answered her own question.

"Why," she said, "my picture just fell off the wall!"

The three boys ran over to where a large painting in a gold frame lay on its side on the floor. As Pete and Jupiter set it upright, they saw that it was a fine picture of Miss Agawam as a young woman.

"The artist who illustrated my books did it many years ago," explained Miss Agawam.

The portrait showed her sitting on the grass reading from a book while many strange little creatures, probably meant to be gnomes and elves, crowded around to listen.

A wire hung from a molding near the ceiling had supported the picture, and this wire had obviously broken. Jupiter examined the break. He looked solemn.

"This wire didn't just break, Miss Agawam," he said. "It was filed almost through, so it had to break sooner or later."

"Oh, dear!" Miss Agawam touched her face with her handkerchief. "The gnomes! They must have done it. The other night when—oh, but I haven't come to that

51

yet."

"I think we can fix the wire for you, Miss Agawam," Jupiter said. "And hang the picture up again. You tell us while we work."

They carefully turned the picture over and Pete, who was very handy at fixing things, knotted the broken wire.

Bob took notes as Miss Agawam continued her story. She had only been locked in the cellar a few moments when her nephew Roger arrived, letting himself in with his own key. She had called out and pounded on the door, and he had released her. But when she told him her story, though he was very nice, she could tell he didn't believe a word of it. Miss Agawam was sure he thought she had been walking in her sleep and dreamed the whole thing.

"Excuse us a moment, Miss Agawam," Jupiter requested, "and we'll hang up the picture again."

Pete stood on a chair, and Jupiter handed the portrait up to him. As he did so, Bob saw Jupe's eyes suddenly gleam with excitement. Bob knew what that meant.

Jupe had had an idea!

"What is it, Jupe?" Bob whispered, as Pete climbed down.

Jupe was looking rather self-satisfied.

"I believe I have solved the riddle of the Golden Belt!" he whispered back.

"You have? Golly, what's the answer?" Bob had to stop himself from yelling the words. "How could you solve it now, here, anyway?"

"A clue is a clue, wherever you find it," Jupe said under his breath. "We will talk about it later. Right now we have a duty to help Miss Agawam."

Bob sighed. He knew Jupe wouldn't say another word until he was good and ready. He tried to imagine what clue Jupiter might have come across, but he couldn't. So he gave his full attention to Miss Agawam as she took up her story once more.

"Roger wanted me to come to stay at his apartment, but I wouldn't," she said. "He waited awhile, but we heard nothing more, so he left.

"Well, nothing more happened that night. But the next night I heard strange noises again. I suppose I should have phoned Roger, but his attitude that first night—telling me I must have had a bad dream—well, I didn't like it. I didn't want him thinking I was hearing and seeing things.

"I slipped downstairs very carefully, just in time to hear the back door close. In the library here some of my pictures had been thrown on the floor. All my books had been taken out of the shelves and pages had been torn out of some. As if the gnomes wanted to be nasty and unpleasant. That must have been when they filed the wire of my picture.

"I was very upset. I did phone Roger in the morning and he came over. But he wouldn't believe that gnomes had done it all. He very tactfully told me that I must have done it myself, and he thought I should go away somewhere for a good rest. I practically ordered him out of the house. Because I know it really happened! I am definitely not walking in my sleep and having delusions!

"But what does it all *mean*?" Miss Agawam asked, wringing her hands. "It's all so mysterious. I can't understand a single bit of it!"

Neither could Pete or Bob. Looking at Miss Agawam, they found it hard not to believe that every word she spoke was the truth. At the same time, her story seemed too preposterous to be true.

"The first thing to do," Jupiter said finally—for it was obvious he didn't have any handy answers either— "is to get evidence that these gnomes really do exist and are bothering you, Miss Agawam."

"Yes, of course!" she clasped her hands. "Then we can learn why."

"What we have to do is set a trap for them," Jupiter told her.

"What kind of trap?" Pete asked.

"A human trap," Jupe replied. "One of us will spend the night here and try to catch one of them."

"Oh we will, will we? Which one of us?"

"You, Pete. You're the one I had in mind."

"Now wait a minute!" Pete protested. "I don't want to be a human gnome trap. It's a line of work I don't care for. Even though I don't believe in gnomes, I don't believe in taking chances, either."

"We have to station someone here who is strong, swift, and courageous," Jupiter said. "I'm strong and fairly courageous, but I'm not very swift. Bob is fast, now that his brace has been taken off his leg—" he was referring to a brace Bob had worn for some years on a leg badly broken when he was a small boy—"and he has the courage of a lion. But he is not as strong as we are.

"No, Pete, the only one of us who is strong, fast and courageous is you."

Pete swallowed hard. What do you do when someone tells you you're courageous but you don't feel a bit courageous yourself?

"Why don't we all stay?" he asked. "Three heads are better than one. We can take turns staying awake."

"I'm supposed to go with my mother and father to visit my aunt tonight," Bob said. "That lets me out."

"You haven't any excuse, Jupe," Pete told him. "Tomorrow is Sunday so the salvage yard won't be open. Suppose you and I stay?"

Jupiter pinched his lip.

"Well, all right," he said. "Perhaps that is a better idea. No doubt two of us can handle the situation better than one. Will it be all right, Miss Agawam, if Pete and I spend the night here with you?"

"Oh, would you?" Miss Agawam exclaimed in delight. "I'll be so pleased. There's a room at the head of the stairs you can have. You're sure you don't mind? I don't want to get you into any danger."

"The gnomes haven't hurt you, Miss Agawam," Jupiter said. "I don't think they plan any harm. But we must see them, and capture one if possible, to find out what's going on. Tonight, after dark, we will come back and wait. We will try to slip in unseen so no one will know that reinforcements have arrived."

"That'll be wonderful," Miss Agawam said. "I'll be waiting for you. Just press the bell and I'll open the gate lock."

When they were out in the street again Pete burst out, "Well, is she just imagining things, Jupe? That's what I want to know."

"I don't know," Jupiter said, thoughtfully. "She might be. But she doesn't act like a lady who imagines things. Maybe she really has seen some gnomes."

"Aw, come on!" Pete scoffed. "Nobody believes in gnomes any more."

"Some people do," Jupiter told him. "Just as some people believe in ghosts."

"Just a few years ago, in 1938," Bob piped up, "some scientists discovered a strange fish that was supposed to have been extinct for a million years. It's called a coelacanth. Now scientists know there are thousands, maybe millions of them in the seas.

"Why—" Bob was just getting warmed up—"suppose there really is a race of little people who are called gnomes or goblins or elves. Suppose a long time ago they had to hide underground because bigger people wanted to kill them and eat them. Then they really could exist just as the coelacanth did, only nobody's caught one yet."

"Excellent thinking," Jupiter said. "A good investigator must take every possibility into account. Tonight we will come prepared for anything."

He stood looking down the street. Pete was getting restless.

"Come on," he said. "Let's get in the truck and get back home. It's dinner time and I'm hungry."

"I think we should walk around the block first," Jupiter said. "We inspected the hedge and fence from the inside, but not from the outside."

"You mean to see if there is any place a gnome could get out?" Bob asked.

"Certainly," Jupiter answered. "Perhaps closer inspection will reveal something we missed."

They started toward the old movie house on the corner, Pete still grumbling that he was hungry.

The doors to the theater were boarded over and covered with tattered advertising signs. They walked around the corner and down one long side of the building, until they came to an alley.

"This alley runs behind Miss Agawam's house," Jupiter said. "We'll go down it and inspect her fence."

A few feet down the narrow passageway, they passed a metal door set into the back of the old theater. In faded letters it said "Stage Door." It was open a couple of inches and, unexpectedly, they heard a rumble of voices inside.

"That's odd," Jupiter said. "The signs out front say 'Closed' and 'Positively No Admittance'."

"I wonder what it's like inside?" Pete was beginning to get interested. "I bet it's pretty spooky."

Jupiter sat down on the stone step outside the door and began to tie and untie his shoelaces, trying to hear what was being said inside. All he could make out was a rumble of voices, as of two men talking.

"Listen!" Pete began.

"Sssh!" Jupiter said tensely. "I just heard someone say the words 'Golden Belt.' "

"Golden Belt! Golly!" Bob whispered. "Do you suppose——"

"Quiet!" Jupiter was listening intently. "I just heard the word 'museum.' "

"Gosh, maybe we've stumbled on the thieves' hideout!" Pete whispered, eyes round. "Wouldn't that be something!"

"We must try to hear more before we call the police," Jupiter murmured.

All three boys moved nearer the door. Clearly they heard the word "museum" spoken again. Almost bursting with eagerness, they crowded closer. The door, not really shut, swung open and all three boys sprawled headlong into the hall inside.

As they tried to get to their feet, large hands grasped their collars and a deep voice bellowed in their ears.

"Trespassers!" it roared. "Mr. Jordan, send for the cops! I've nabbed some kids breaking in!"

Chapter Seven

Inside the Old Theater

A heavy-set man with dark eyebrows and a ferocious scowl on his face hauled Pete and Bob to their feet.

"I've got you!" he growled. "Don't try to get away! Mr. Jordan, there's one more. You grab him!"

"Run, Jupe!" Pete gasped. "Get Hans!"

Jupiter, however, stood his ground.

"You're making a mistake," he said in his most adult manner. "Hearing voices within a supposedly empty and abandoned structure, we were under the impression that there were trespassers inside, and we were endeavoring to make sure of our suspicions before contacting the authorities."

"Huh?" The heavy-set man stared at him, mouth open. "What'd you say?"

It was a trick Jupe sometimes used, which almost always gave adults a jolt of surprise.

Now another man appeared behind the first one. He was younger, thinner and light-haired.

"Relax, Rawley," he said, looking amused. "The boy simply said he heard our voices and thought we were trespassers. They were trying to make sure before calling the police."

"If that's what he meant, why didn't he say so?" demanded Rawley, who seemed to have a bad disposition. "I hate smart-aleck kids who talk like dictionaries."

"I'm Frank Jordan, owner of this theater," the other man told them. "That is, I bought it in order to tear it down and build a new office building. I was just checking with Rawley, here, my night watchman. Why did you boys think our conversation sounded suspicious?"

"The building is supposed to be all locked up——" Jupiter began, but Pete, indignant about the way he had been grabbed, burst out, "We heard you talking about the Golden Belt! That's why we were suspicious. Especially when you mentioned the museum too!"

Rawley's face darkened again.

"Mr. Jordan!" he said. "These kids are screwballs! Troublemakers. I say we call the cops!"

"I'm in charge here, Rawley," Mr. Jordan told him. He looked puzzled, however, by Pete's statement. "Golden Belt?" he said. "I don't remember mentioning any such thing."

Then his face cleared and he smiled.

"Oh, so that's it!" he said. "Now I remember. As I said, I'm going to tear this old theater down. I was telling Rawley that the inside is so elaborate, with so much gold and gilt, that it's like a museum. I said I really hated to tear it down.

"You see? 'Gold and gilt,' if not heard clearly, could easily sound like 'Golden Belt.' You boys have been reading too much about that museum robbery."

He chuckled. Rawley, however, still looked menacing.

"They got too much imagination," he muttered.

"Lucky you don't have any imagination," his employer told him. "You aren't bothered by any of those mysterious noises that made my last two night watchmen quit."

"Mysterious noises?" Jupiter asked, suddenly interested. "What kind of noises?"

"Mysterious knocks and muffled groans," Mr. Jordan said. "But there are logical explanations. It's certainly spooky enough inside, I admit, but that's because it is so big and dark. When it was new it was a very beautiful place.

"Maybe you boys would like to look around inside and see that gold and gilt I was talking about?" he asked, smiling.

Eagerly, they said they would.

"Turn on the main lights, Rawley," Mr. Jordan directed, and led the boys down a dark narrow hall, lit by just a single bulb.

The farther they went, the thicker the darkness grew. Something brushed past Bob's face and he let out a yell.

"A bat!" he cried.

"I'm afraid so," Mr. Jordan's voice came out of the darkness. "This theater has been empty so long it has many bats in it. Rats, too. Enormous ones."

Bob gulped but kept silent as he heard the whir of leathery wings in the air over his head. Then he heard strange creakings and groanings ahead, and he felt as if his hair was standing on end.

"Those noises," Mr. Jordan said, "are just the old ropes and pulleys once used to hang the scenery. Besides being a movie theater, this place presented vaudeville shows. Ah, I see Rawley has found the light."

A dim light relieved the darkness as the boys emerged on the stage of the theater. From here they could look out over what seemed miles of empty seats. Overhead, an enormous chandelier of colored glass—green and red and yellow and blue—shone dustily.

Red plush curtains, heavy with gilt fringe, hung at the side windows. The walls were liberally decorated with scenes of knights and Saracens fighting, all in gold armor. As Mr. Jordan had said, there was lots of gold and gilt around, and the inside did have a museum-like atmosphere.

"This theater was built during the nineteen-twenties," Mr. Jordan said, "when people felt a movie theater should look like a palace or a castle. This one was made to look like a Moorish mosque. You should see the funny stairways, and the minarets on the roof. Ah well, times change."

He turned to lead them back to the alley. A shadowy gray form scampered across the stage in front of them.

"One of our resident rats," Mr. Jordan said. "They've had the place all to themselves for years. They won't like being evicted. Well, here you are, boys. Now you know what the old Moorish Theater looks like. Come watch us tear it down in a few weeks."

He ushered them out into the alley and the door closed behind them. Firmly. They heard it lock.

"Wow!" Pete said. "Bats and rats! No wonder night watchmen wouldn't stay."

"Presumably they are responsible for the mysterious knocks and groans," Jupe said. "I admit that when I overheard what sounded like 'Golden Belt' I felt sure we had stumbled on an important clue to the museum case. However, Mr. Jordan's explanation is very logical and I believe it."

"It would have been nice if we could have nabbed the museum robbers after being chased off the case," Pete sighed. "But I guess that's asking too much."

"I'm afraid it is," Jupiter agreed. "Let's not forget we're trying to help Miss Agawam. So come on and we'll finish our inspection of the alley."

They walked on down the alley, testing the boards of the high fence which walled off the rear of Miss Agawam's property. Every one was solid. The gate was tightly locked.

"Nobody could have gotten in or out this way," Jupiter remarked, pinching his lip. "It's all very curious."

"I'm more hungry than I am curious," Pete said. "Can't we go home now?"

"Yes, I guess there's nothing more we can do now," Jupiter agreed.

They walked back to the truck, where Hans was patiently reading a newspaper, and piled in.

As the truck moved through the city traffic, Bob wanted to ask a question. He wanted to ask Jupiter what clue he had suddenly found, or remembered, back in Miss Agawam's house that had made him say he had solved the riddle of the Golden Belt.

But Jupiter had settled back with his "thinking look" on his face, and Bob knew he wouldn't want to be inter-rupted now with questions.

So he didn't ask.

Chapter Eight

An Unexpected Visitor

When the truck got back to Rocky Beach and The Jones Salvage Yard, Pete hopped out.

"Got to get home," he said. "I just remembered. It's Dad's birthday and Mom is having a special dinner. I'll be back as soon as I can."

"Try to be here by eight," Jupiter told him. "And be sure to get permission to spend the night with me at the home of a friend of Mr. Hitchcock's. Say we expect to be back tomorrow morning."

"Right." Pete got on his bike and pedaled off.

As Bob and Jupiter climbed out, Jupiter's aunt came out of the neat little cabin that served as an office for the yard.

"You have a visitor, Jupiter," she said. "He's been waiting for half an hour."

"A visitor?" Jupe repeated, surprised. "Who is he?"

"His name is Taro Togati and he's a Japanese boy. But he speaks quite good English. He's been telling me all about how they make cultured pearls. They use trained oysters, or something!"

She gave a deep laugh. She was a cheerful, good-natured woman, though she did have a peculiar fondness for seeing Jupiter and his friends working hard.

"I'll see him in a moment, Aunt Mathilda," Jupiter said. "May I have permission to spend the night with Pete at the home of a friend of Mr. Hitchcock's? She's a lady writer who has been hearing peculiar noises at night."

"Peculiar noises? Well, I guess it will be all right if it makes her feel better to have two big, strong boys in the house." Mrs. Jones laughed again. "All right, Jupiter, you can go down in the truck and call Hans to pick you up in the morning."

She raised her voice. "Jupiter and Bob are here, Taro," she called. Then she added to the boys, "Supper in half an hour," and started off toward the Jones's home.

A small boy, no bigger than Bob, but dressed very neatly in a dark blue suit and tie, came out of the office. He wore gold-rimmed eyeglasses and his hair was combed straight.

"So happy to meet you, Jupiter-san," he said, with a slight accent. "And Bob-san. I am Taro, humble son of Saito Togati, chief detective for Nagasami Jewelry Company."

"Hello, Taro," Jupiter said, shaking hands. "We met your father yesterday."

Taro Togati looked unhappy. From his pocket he took a business card, slightly crumpled.

"Yes, I know," he said. "I am afraid my honorable father was rude. But he is very upset, very distracted. I pick up your card, learn your name. I saw you help people out the door, and I told my father. He asked me to come and give you thanks and many apologies."

"That's all right, Taro," Bob put in. "We know he was upset. And I suppose we are pretty young to be chasing jewel thieves. Right now we're working on a case of mysterious gnomes."

"Gnomes?" Taro Togati's eyes widened. "Oh, I know what you mean. The Small People who dig for treasure underground. I have never seen one, but in Japan we have legends about them. They are most dangerous. Do not let them catch you."

"We would like to catch one of them," said Jupiter. "To see if they actually exist, as the legends say."

As they talked, Jupiter pulled out some rusty iron garden chairs, and they all sat down.

"Tell me, Taro," Jupiter said, with suppressed eagerness, "has your father found the Golden Belt yet?"

"Alas, Jupiter-san," Taro Togati sighed, "my father, guards and police do not yet catch thieves or find Golden Belt. No—what is the word?—no clues. My father is deeply ashamed. Under his nose Golden Belt was stolen, and if he does not get it back, he is dishonored and must resign his job."

"That's tough, Taro," Bob said sympathetically.

Jupiter was pinching his lip, as his mental machinery moved into high gear. "Tell us what actually has been learned, Taro," he said.

Taro described the police's extensive questioning of everyone who had seemed in any way suspicious. All this had not come up with a single likely suspect, nor could they discover how the belt had been removed from the museum. Taro's father and the police had decided that the thieves had taken the Golden Belt, rather than the Rainbow Jewels, because it was in a side case, while the Rainbow Jewels were out in the middle and had been surrounded at the first alarm. Of course, it was less valuable than the Rainbow Jewels, and much harder to get out of the museum, but it was easier to steal.

"But who the thieves were, or how they got the belt out of the museum, no one can guess," Taro said unhappily.

"The guards!" Bob burst out. "One of them could be the thief. He could easily have hidden the belt by letting it hang down inside his pants leg and holding it with his own belt."

"All guards especially hired." Taro said. "My father questioned each. Unless he was deceived. It is possible. I will mention it to him."

"What about Mr. Frank, the actor?" Jupiter asked. "The one who dropped that imitation jewel."

Taro told them that at first the police had been sure Mr. Frank was in on the robbery plot. However, the actor's story was very simple. A woman had hired him by telephone to appear at the museum, and, at exactly noon, drop a large imitation stone from his pocket and look guilty.

She had told him it was a publicity stunt. Of course everyone in Hollywood was familiar with stunts to get publicity, and accepted them as a matter of course. The woman had promised Mr. Frank that if he could get his name in the papers, together with the fact that he was soon to start work on a movie called "The Great Museum Robbery," he would actually get an important part in the picture.

Mr. Frank had agreed. The large fake jewel and a fifty-dollar bill had come to him by mail, and he had just carried out his assignment. It was obvious, Taro said, that the thieves had hired Mr. Frank to provide a moment's distraction just before the actual robbery. But apparently he was innocent of being part of the gang.

Jupe had the slightly smug look he sometimes got when he felt he had a good idea.

"As I thought." He nodded. "And, of course, the police and your father deduced that the thieves purposely chose Children's Day as an ideal time to stage their daring robbery?"

"Ah, so." Taro nodded. "But my father is still much puzzled about how belt was taken outside."

Jupiter looked important.

"It wasn't taken out," he said, exploding a small bombshell of surprise. "It's still in the museum!"

"Still in the museum!" Bob yelped.

"But museum was searched, bottom to top!" Taro protested. "Belt was not found. Offices searched, washrooms searched, every place! Please explain idea, Jupiter-san."

"Today," Jupiter said, "while working on another case, I came across a clue that I think explains the riddle of the disappearance of the Golden Belt. Given the facts as we know them, it seems to me the answer must be——"

He paused. Bob and Taro waited breathlessly.

"Bob," Jupiter said, "you remember when Miss Agawam's picture fell down? Pete and I hung it back up."

Bob nodded. "Sure," he said. "Go on, Jupe."

"As I held the picture, which was quite a large one," Jupiter said, "I noticed that in the back there was a space a couple of inches deep between the actual painting and the outer frame. Now there are many large pictures hanging in the Peterson Museum. I deduce——"

Seeing what he was getting at, Bob finished for him: "Some of those pictures probably have big crevices between the pictures and the carved frames!" he said. "Someone could have slipped the belt behind one of them in the confusion and darkness!"

"Or it could be a gang working together," Jupe said. "We know a woman phoned Mr. Frank. She may have been an accomplice of the actual thief."

Taro Togati leaped excitedly to his feet.

"I am sure men did not look behind pictures when museum was searched!" he said. "I will tell my father this idea at once."

"Whoever hid it probably intends to go back and get it when things have quieted down," Jupiter said. "But as the museum has been closed, it couldn't have been retrieved yet. Tell your father not to skip the balcony, either."

"But the balcony was closed," Taro objected.

"Only by a rope anyone could step over. A picture on the balcony would be an ideal hiding place, as it would seem the least likely."

"Thank you, Jupiter-san!" Taro cried, his eyes shining. "I believe your idea is most excellent one. Excuse me now, I go back at once to tell my father of your thoughts."

They exchanged rapid good-byes and Taro ran out to a

waiting car.

Bob turned to Jupe admiringly.

"Golly, that was sharp thinking, Jupe," he said. "Maybe you've solved the theft of the Golden Belt even though Mr. Togati wouldn't let us work on the case."

For a moment Jupiter looked doubtful. "There may be another answer," he said. "But—no, given all the facts as we have learned them, that is the only explanation which fits. Since the belt wasn't taken outside, it must still be in the museum. The only unsearched spot is behind a picture. I can't find any flaw in my logic."

"It's good enough for me!" Bob said loyally.

"Well, we'll know in the morning," Jupiter said. "Now I have to get together a kit of gnome-catching equipment to take to Miss Agawam's house. Tomorrow morning I will telephone a message to your home. You can come down with Hans to pick us up."

Bob shook his head in perplexity.

"Do you really think you're going to catch a gnome, Jupe?" he asked. "Or do you think Miss Agawam's nephew was right, that she's been walking in her sleep and imagining it all?"

"I'm keeping an open mind," Jupiter told him. "People have done strange things in their sleep. One man who was worried about some jewelry in his safe is known to have walked in his sleep, opened the safe, taken out the jewelry, and hidden it where he couldn't find it himself when he woke up the next morning.

"If Miss Agawam is doing something like that, Pete and I will be witnesses and will be able to convince her of the truth in some way. On the other hand—" and

Jupe's eyes gleamed as he spoke—"if she has been seeing gnomes, or something like gnomes, we'll be all set to catch one!"

Chapter Nine

Start of a Gnome Hunt

The gnomes were digging busily. Far down at the end of the rocky underground tunnel, Bob could see tiny forms swinging pickaxes.

He crept forward, wishing Pete and Jupiter were with him. He didn't want to go any deeper into that tunnel, where the darkness was so black, but now that he was this close, he couldn't let The Three Investigators down.

His heart pounding, he moved closer, until he was crouching just outside the cavelike room where the gnomes were working. Then, because of the dust in the air, he sneezed.

Instantly, every gnome stopped working exactly as he was, some with pickaxes raised over their heads. They all turned slowly, very slowly.

Bob wanted to run, but the instant their eyes were on him, he was rooted to the spot as if by some kind of magic. He couldn't utter a sound.

They stared at him without moving. Then he heard footsteps behind him. Something very strange and scary was sneaking up on him. He tried to turn and look—but he couldn't move.

A big claw dropped on his shoulder and shook him.

"Bob!" a voice boomed, hollow and echoing in the cave. "Bob! Wake up!"

The sound broke the spell. Bob squirmed and started to shout.

"Let me go!" he yelled. "Let me go!"

Then he blinked. He was lying in his own bed and his mother was looking down at him.

"Why, Bob, were you having a dream?" his mother asked. "You were wriggling around and muttering strangely in your sleep. So I woke you."

"Golly, yes, I guess it was a dream, all right," Bob said thankfully. "Jupiter didn't call, did he?"

"Jupiter? Why should Jupiter call at this time of night? You've only been asleep a few minutes. Now go back to sleep and please try not to dream."

"I will, Mom."

Bob turned over to sleep again, wondering how Jupiter and Pete were making out.

At that moment, the two boys were riding in the pickup truck on their way to Miss Agawam's home. As they rode, Jupe showed Pete the equipment he had assembled in his gnome-catching kit.

"Most important, the camera," he began. It was Jupe's pride, a special camera that developed a picture within ten seconds. It was a rather expensive make, but Jupe had obtained it in broken condition from a boy at school, trading him a repaired bicycle for it.

"For taking instant pictures of gnomes or anything else we meet tonight," Jupe explained. "Here's the flashbulb attachment."

He replaced the camera and took out two pairs of work gloves with leather palms.

"Gloves for handling gnomes," he said. "They are supposed to have strong teeth and sharp nails. These will help protect our hands."

"Golly," Pete said, "you act as if you really expect to catch some gnomes."

"It always pays to be prepared," Jupiter told him. "Now the rope.

"A hundred feet of light nylon, very strong. In fact, almost unbreakable," Jupe said. "It should be enough to tie up any gnomes we can catch."

Next he brought out two home-built walkie-talkies that had been added to their equipment some time before. Though their range was short, these instruments enabled the boys to keep in touch while on a case. They were especially proud of this professional touch.

"Flashlights," Jupiter said, taking out two powerful ones. "And finally the tape recorder. For recording any sounds of digging," Jupiter said. He studied the kit and nodded.

"All seems to be complete," he said. "Do you have your special chalk?"

Pete produced a stick of blue chalk from his pocket. Jupiter took out his white chalk. Bob's stick was green. By simply scrawling ? or ? ? ? somewhere in green, blue or white, the boys could let each other know they had been there, or were inside, or had found something at the spot worth investigating.

The rest of the world would think nothing of scrawled

question marks in chalk, considering them the work of children at play. It was one of Jupiter's most ingenious devices.

"I believe we are now all set," Jupiter said. "Did you bring a toothbrush?"

Pete held up a small zipper bag.

"Toothbrush and pajamas," he said.

"I don't think we will need the pajamas," Jupiter said. "We will remain fully clothed, ready to catch a gnome."

Hans looked sharply across at the two boys.

"You are still chasing gnomes, Jupe?" Hans asked. "Konrad and I, we think you should not mess around with gnomes. Many bad stories about them are told in the Black Forest of Bavaria. Stay away from them, that is what Konrad says. That is what I say. That is what we both say. Or else you will, perhaps, be turned into rocks!"

Hans sounded so positive that Pete couldn't help feeling a little uneasy. Of course there weren't any gnomes, but just the same, Hans and Konrad believed in them, Miss Agawam believed in them, and who could tell, just maybe——

Jupiter spoke, interrupting Pete's thoughts. "We have promised to assist Miss Agawam in her present difficulties," he said. "I don't know whether she is really being bothered by gnomes or not but, in any case, you remember the motto of The Three Investigators."

" 'We Investigate Anything'," Pete muttered.

Secretly he wondered if that didn't include just a little too much territory!

Chapter Ten

Trapped!

It was dark and still on Miss Agawam's block. The closed bank and the deserted theater were pitch-black, and only a single light burning in the house told them Miss Agawam was waiting for them.

As Pete and Jupiter started to climb out, Hans looked at them with a worried frown.

"I still say you should not try to catch gnomes, Jupe," he said. "In the Black Forest where I grow up are many strange rocks and stumps that once were people. It is because they look at a gnome, eye to eye. You better watch out!"

Pete didn't care for this line of conversation. Hans sounded so positive. His feeling of nervousness came back. Something told him the night ahead was going to bring some very unexpected surprises.

Jupe said good night hastily, promising that he would phone Hans in the morning, and the truck pulled away.

Keeping to the shadows along the fence, the boys made their way down the sidewalk to Miss Agawam's gate. No one, as far as they could detect, was watching them.

Jupiter gave the bell at the gate three short pushes.

Instantly the lock buzzed. They slipped quickly inside and Jupiter paused to listen. Pete was puzzled. The way Jupe was acting you would think he was on a secret mission involving the fate of great armies. But then, Jupe never was careless on a case.

Also, Jupe liked to make things dramatic.

Inside the gate, the yard was in darkness. Silently they stole up on the porch, the door opened, and they slipped inside.

Miss Agawam, a bit pale, greeted them.

"I'm so glad you're here," she said. "The truth is, for the first time in my life I was feeling very nervous. I do believe that if anything more should happen, I would just run out of here and never come back! I'd sell the house to that Mr. Jordan who wants it so badly."

"We are here, and we will take charge, Miss Agawam," Jupiter said politely.

Miss Agawam smiled, a bit shakily. "It's still quite early," she said. "I never have noticed any digging or other activities before midnight. Would you like to look at television?"

"I believe we will take a short nap until eleven-thirty," Jupiter said. "That way we will be refreshed for the night's vigil."

"What's a vigil?" Pete asked.

"It means we stay awake and watch for whatever happens. Miss Agawam, do you have an alarm clock?"

Miss Agawam nodded. She showed Pete and Jupiter to the small room at the head of the stairs where two beds were made up. The boys took off their shoes, made sure their equipment was ready, and stretched out.

In spite of his uneasiness, Pete fell asleep easily. Sleeping was one thing he never had trouble doing. But it seemed no time at all before a small bell roused him.

"What's 'at?" he muttered, still half asleep.

"It's eleven-thirty," Jupe whispered. "Miss Agawam has retired to her room. You can sleep. I'll keep watch."

"Vigil," Pete muttered and was asleep again.

Unlike Bob, Pete almost never dreamed. But now he began to dream it was hailing and the hail was tapping on the windows.

He woke up, this time quite alert, and lay still for a moment. The tapping continued. Pete realized someone actually was tapping on the window. It had a curious rhythm: one—three—two—three—one. Like a code. Or like a magical formula.

With that thought he sat bolt upright, staring at the window. His heart did a double flip-flop and seemed to lodge in his throat.

There was a face peering in at the window!

It was a tiny face, with small, glaring eyes, hairy ears, and a long pointed nose. Small lips drew back and fang-like teeth snarled at him.

The room all around him suddenly was lit by a flash of lightning, and Pete jumped.

But there was no thunder. The face at the window instantly vanished, and Pete realized the light had come from a camera flashbulb.

"Got him!" Jupiter exclaimed in the darkness. "You awake, Pete?"

"Sure I'm awake!" Pete exclaimed. "That was a gnome looking in at us!"

"And I have a photograph of him. Now let's see if we can catch him."

Both boys crowded to the window. They blinked, trying hard to see. Out in the yard, four tiny figures in tall peaked caps were dancing around crazily. They turned somersaults. One stood on another's shoulders and turned a backward somersault. They played leapfrog. They looked like children playing some wild game.

As his eyes grew accustomed to the dark, Pete could even see their tiny white faces, their pointed shoes, their leather clothing.

"Golly, Jupe!" he whispered. "There are four of them! But why are they doing tricks in the yard like that?"

"I think the answer is clear," Jupiter replied, pulling on his shoes. "They are hoping to scare us and Miss Agawam."

"Scare us?" Pete said. "Well, they've made me nervous, if that's what they want. But why should they want to scare us and Miss Agawam? What about the digging?"

"Merely an extra added detail. I deduce, Pete, that the gnomes have been hired by Miss Agawam's nephew, Roger."

"Hired by Roger!" Pete repeated, lacing on his shoes. "What for?"

"To scare her into selling this house and moving away. Remember, she told us Roger was very anxious for her to sell and move into a little apartment. She also told us Roger is her only relative. That means he's her heir— someday he will inherit all her money."

A great light burst in Pete's mind.

"I get it!" he said. "If she sells now she'll get a lot of

money which he'll inherit some day. He wants her to sell to Mr. Jordan—sure! So he hired the gnomes to scare her. Jupe, you're a genius!"

"In order to prove anything," Jupiter said, "we have to catch at least one of these creatures and make him talk."

Jupe grabbed the rope from the emergency kit and thrust it through his belt. He pulled on a pair of work gloves, tossed a pair to Pete, and slung his ten-second camera over his shoulder. They both attached flashlights to their belts to keep their hands free.

"How could the gnome look in the window? It's on the second floor," Pete asked as they hurried.

"Figure it out, Pete. You need the experience in simple deduction," Jupiter said. "Come on. Miss Agawam must still be asleep. That's good. We don't want to alarm her."

They slipped down the stairs and out the front door. Silently as shadows, they eased off the porch to the corner of the house. On their knees, they peeked around.

The four strange little men were still doing wild acrobatics in the yard—turning somersaults and cartwheels, playing leapfrog.

"Here!" Jupe gave Pete one end of the rope. The other end he tied around his wrist. "Rush them. Get the rope around one and wrap it tight. Come on!"

They made a dash for it. As they burst from cover, Jupiter's camera strap caught on the branch of a bush, and the camera was ripped from his shoulder. But Jupiter did not pause.

The gnomes saw them coming. With a shrill whistle, they scattered and ran headlong toward the deeper darkness of a shadow along the brick wall.

"After them!" Jupiter gasped. "Catch at least one!"

"I'm trying!" Pete panted. His fingers almost closed on the shoulder of one tiny figure. But the little man ducked, and Pete went headlong on the ground. Jupiter fell over him. As they picked themselves up, they saw the four little creatures disappearing into a dark opening in the wall of the theater.

"The door!" Jupe gasped. "It's open now."

"They went inside. Now we've got them!" Pete cried. "Come on, Jupe."

He ran headlong for the open door.

"Wait, Pete!" Jupiter yelled, holding back. "I've had time to think some more and now I deduce——"

But Pete wasn't listening. He had already rushed through the open emergency door. He held tight to the rope Jupe had tied to his own wrist, and his speed pulled Jupe along behind him.

Jupiter, running as fast as he could to keep from falling on his face, ran through the door and into the pitch darkness inside the great building.

The instant they were both inside, the door closed with an iron bang. They were trapped!

And a second later small creatures with sharp nails were attacking them from all sides.

Chapter Eleven

A Wild Chase

"Help!" shouted Pete. "The gnomes have me!"

"They've got me, too!" Jupiter grunted, trying to brush off the small creatures who seemed to be swarming all over him. "They trapped us!"

He swung his arm. The rope was still tied to his wrist and Pete still held the other end. It caught some small creature in the neck. They heard a gurgle and a shrill scream and the tiny man went flying.

Jupiter was free. But the gnomes would return to the attack. He could hear Pete grunting and thrashing around nearby. Jupiter reached out, got a good hold of a leather jacket and pulled. The little man came loose and Jupiter swung him through the air and let him go.

He came down with a satisfying thud and a high-pitched squeal.

With Jupiter's help, Pete tossed off his other attacker and the two boys pressed close together in the darkness, panting. Jupe untied the rope and put it in his pocket.

"What do we do now, Jupe?" Pete gasped.

"Try to find the door we came in and go back out," Jupe said. "It's behind us—this way, I think."

They backed up until they bumped against a wall. Jupe felt around and found the handle of the iron door. He rattled it but the door wouldn't budge. They were locked in!

"We're trapped all right." Jupe's voice was glum. "Why did you have to rush in so fast, Pete? You should have guessed that's what they wanted us to do."

"I thought I had them," Pete confessed. "And I just pulled you along after me, didn't I?"

"Yes," Jupe answered. "And that's what they wanted. To get us inside. And now—listen!"

In the darkness, they heard shrill whistles to the right and left of them.

"They're getting ready to attack again!" Pete exclaimed.

"We have to get out of here!" Jupiter said. "Maybe we can force our way out the front of the theater."

"How can we find it in this darkness?"

"Our flashlights. In our excitement, we have been forgetting them. That is one effect of fright—it clouds the thinking processes."

Pete slapped his leg. His flashlight was still clipped to his belt. He thumbed it on, and a beam of light shot out, cutting the darkness. A second later Jupiter's light was added to his.

Tiny figures tumbled for cover as the light hit them, and small voices chattered in a shrill, strange language. Apparently the gnomes were more wary now. They knew Pete and Jupiter were not to be overcome so easily.

The two boys were in the backstage region of the movie house. Here, large rectangular canvas "flats" were stacked in rows, left over from the days when the theater had shown vaudeville and even an occasional play. A sagging couch, an old spinning wheel, a step-ladder stood just where they had been left when the building had closed many years ago.

And there was the whisper of wings in the air. Something dark flashed past their heads and was gone.

"Bats!" Pete yelled.

"Never mind the bats. We're going to be attacked," Jupiter said. The little men were creeping up, now armed with pieces of wood for clubs. "Where shall we go?"

"This way. Follow me."

Pete dashed off. He was an expert at finding his way, even in strange surroundings. He had an instinct like a built-in compass for going in the right direction.

Pete ran along between two rows of stacked canvas flats. Jupiter followed, kicking over the stepladder behind him.

Shrill squeals told him one of their pursuers had gotten tangled in the ladder. But an instant later Pete stopped so suddenly Jupe ran into him. Down at the other end of the narrow alley, two tiny men armed with clubs were waiting for them.

"We're cornered," Pete gulped. "They're in back of us and in front of us."

"Then we have to go sideways," Jupiter said. "Make a hole in the canvas."

He kicked. The old rotted canvas gave way like paper and Jupiter and Pete ducked through. More scenery flats were in their way. Now they just put their heads down and rammed through like bulldozers, leaving ragged, flapping canvas behind them.

Soon their pursuers were lost in the canvas scenery behind them. Jupiter and Pete, still running, came out on the big wooden stage of the theater.

They beamed their lights outward. Beyond the hundreds of empty, dusty seats, far in the distance, were the doorways that might lead to the outside. That is, if they could get through the barricades they knew nailed the outer doors shut.

As they were studying the situation, light footsteps sounded behind them. Pete swung his flashlight. The gnomes were creeping up on them.

"Keep going," Pete yelled. "Up the center aisle."

He dashed for the steps which led to the main floor of the theater. At that moment the lights overhead came on —someone had pushed the main switch.

The big green and red chandelier glowed dimly. As he followed Pete down the stairs, Jupe saw two tiny figures coming for him. One of them grabbed a rope hanging down from overhead. Like an acrobat, he sailed through the air and dropped squarely on Jupe's shoulders. Jupiter went down, losing his flashlight, fighting for dear life to pull loose the gnome who now sat on his shoulders.

Pete ran to Jupiter's aid, grabbing the tiny man around the waist and pulling him loose from the First Investigator. He dumped him head first between the first two rows of seats, where he got stuck and squealed for help.

The other little men stopped running long enough to pull him free, and Bob and Pete used that chance to dash up the main aisle into the lobby.

They ran full force against the big main doors. But the doors did not budge.

"They're nailed shut with boards across the outside," Pete gasped. "We'll have to try to find a window or something. Come on, Jupe."

He dashed down a side corridor and up a dark flight of steps. With Pete's flashlight as their only light, they went up one flight of stairs, then another. Stopping to rest, Pete shut off the flash and they peered between some decaying velvet curtains.

Apparently they had climbed up to the level of the balcony. They could see, far below them, four tiny figures huddled in consultation.

As they watched, another figure came down from the stage into the auditorium. He was an ordinary man, heavy-set, and there was just enough light for them to see who he was.

"Rawley!" Pete gasped. "He's working with them!"

"Yes." Jupiter sounded very gloomy. "I made a serious error, Pete. But we haven't time to discuss it now. Listen."

"Hey, Small Fry!" Rawley was bellowing to the four gnomes. "Scatter and find those kids. We have to get them, you hear? They can't go far—every door is nailed shut!"

The four little men below started off obediently in different directions.

"They've lost our trail for the moment," Jupiter said. "If we can find a hiding place, sooner or later Miss Agawam will wake up. Then——"

"Golly, yes! She'll find we're missing and she'll send for the police. The police will search for us! They're bound to look here," Pete said, his spirits suddenly rising.

"They'll find my camera there on the bush," Jupiter said. "They'll pull the film out and know something strange is going on. If we can just hide until Miss Agawam reports us missing, we'll be safe."

"Then let's hunt for a hiding place fast!" Pete said. "I hear voices coming up the stairs."

Chapter Twelve

Pete Climbs for His Life

Miss Agatha Agawam awoke with the sound of digging in her ears. She lay quietly in bed for a moment, listening. Yes, there it was, far underneath her—the gnomes were at it again.

Had the boys heard them? So nice of them to offer to stay with her. There was no sound from their room. Perhaps they were still asleep. Perhaps they had slept right through the alarm.

"Boys!" she called. "Jupiter! Pete!"

There was no reply. She would have to wake them so they could hear the gnomes, too.

Miss Agawam slipped out of bed and put on a woolly robe. She hurried down the hall to the door of their room.

"Boys!" she called again. Still no answer. She opened the door and found the light switch. As the light illuminated the room, Miss Agawam gasped.

The boys' beds were empty!

Her heart pounding, Miss Agawam looked around. Their pajamas, unused, were still neatly folded on a chair. That leather kit they had brought with them was

88

still there.

She jumped to the first conclusion that came to her. Pete and Jupiter had heard the gnomes, been frightened, and had gone home. They had abandoned her.

"Oh, dear," Miss Agawam whispered to herself, "what shall I do now?"

She couldn't stay in that house any longer. She just couldn't. Not after such fine boys as Jupiter Jones and Pete Crenshaw had been so frightened they had run away.

She'd go to her nephew Roger's apartment. He'd invited her to come any time she wanted.

She slipped downstairs to the telephone. Her fingers were shaking so much that she had to try three times to dial his number. When at last his welcome voice answered, she gasped, "The gnomes! They're back. I can hear them plain as plain. Roger, I can't stay here another moment. I want to come to stay with you tonight. Tomorrow—yes, tomorrow I'll sell the house to Mr. Jordan!"

"Auntie dear," Roger boomed, "I think you should sell the house, but we can talk about that tomorrow. You get dressed now and pack a little bag and I'll start right away for you in my car. Be on the sidewalk in ten minutes and I'll be there."

"All right, Roger dear, I'll be ready," Miss Agawam promised.

Feeling better, but with her heart still fluttering, she began to dress. Her nervousness didn't really start to go away until she had left the house, not even checking to make sure the door was locked, and was safely in Roger's car.

Meanwhile, Jupiter and Pete's nervousness was growing stronger.

The boys were still searching for a hiding place in the upper part of the theater. They used the flashlight only when they had to. Mostly they felt their way down dark corridors which smelled of age and dampness and old carpeting.

Behind them, every so often, they could hear the voices of their pursuers. Rawley's bellow seemed to be getting closer.

They came to a door and shoved on it. Jupiter shone his light around. Two very old motion-picture projectors stood in the middle of a dusty little room.

"This was the projection room," Pete gasped. "Let's hide here."

"Too obvious." Jupiter was beginning to look worried. "We'll have to try somewhere else. If Miss Agawam doesn't wake up soon and call the police, we may be in trouble."

"We *may* be in trouble?" Pete repeated. "We *are* in trouble. We'll just be in worse trouble if she doesn't wake up and find us missing."

"Let's keep going," Jupiter said.

They went down the hall and climbed another flight of stairs. These ended on a small platform, against a closed door that said: "Minaret—Do Not Enter."

"What's a minaret?" Pete asked. "Some kind of monster, I bet."

"You're thinking of a minotaur," Jupiter told him. "A minaret is sort of an open tower. Let's try it. I have an idea."

The door was rusted shut, but a good push opened it. Very narrow, steep steps lay behind it. They closed the door, wishing they could lock it, and climbed up the ladder-like steps.

A minute later they came out in a little square tower, open on all four sides, high above the street. Below, everything was dark and deserted, lighted only by the glow of a street lamp.

"Well, we've found the minaret all right," Pete said. "And there's no place to go from here. If you ask me, we're trapped but good!"

"At least we aren't locked in," Jupiter said. "There's the street and safety. All we have to do is reach it. It's only about seventy-five feet away."

"Only seventy-five feet. Straight down. Ha ha!" Pete laughed hollowly.

"We have a rope." Jupiter pulled the coil of light rope from his pocket. "I have here a hundred feet of strong nylon rope. This will easily hold twice your weight."

"Twice *my* weight?" Pete protested. "Why twice *my* weight? Why not twice your weight?"

"Because I am no good at athletics. You are," Jupiter told him. "We'll tie the rope around this corner post, then you will let yourself down and run for the police. We can't wait for Miss Agawam. The pursuit is getting too close."

Pete pulled the rope through his hands.

"It's too thin and slippery," he said. "I couldn't hold on to it. It would cut right into me."

"You have gloves with leather palms. They will help. Wrap the rope around each hand and let it slide slowly through your palms."

Pete tried it. The gloves did help him get a grip on the thin nylon. At last he nodded. It could be done.

"All right," he said. "I'll do it. If you'll tell me just one thing."

"What is that?" Jupiter asked, busily tying one end of the rope to the corner of the minaret.

"We found some genuine gnomes, didn't we?"

"Genuine little people, yes," Jupiter said. "But I was wrong when I said their main purpose was to scare Miss Agawam into selling her house. They really were digging for treasure all along. It was very dense of me not to realize that from the first."

"Realize it?" Pete exclaimed. "How could you? I mean, why should anyone be digging for treasure under Miss Agawam's house?"

"They weren't. Not underneath the house, really." Jupiter sounded as if he thought Pete should have it all figured out for himself by now. "Where is the nearest treasure to here?"

"Oh, some place up in the mountains, I suppose."

"You're not thinking. The nearest treasure is in the bank just on the other side of Miss Agawam's house."

"In the bank?" Pete stared at him. "What do you mean by that?"

"You'd better get started quickly, or they'll find us," Jupiter said impatiently. "Go down as fast as you dare but don't take any chances."

"Don't worry, I won't," Pete said and lowered himself over the side of the narrow minaret.

He had decided to walk himself down—that is, to

plant his feet against the wall, lean back, and walk down a step at a time, letting the rope move slowly through his gloved palms.

He tried not to look down at the hard, dark pavement far below. He concentrated on planting his feet against the rough stucco surface of the theater.

One step at a time he eased himself down. He had progressed nearly halfway to the bottom when he heard shouts up above him. Jupiter yelled, a deep voice grunted, then there was silence. Pete's heart thudded. Had they found Jupiter up there? If so he had better hurry and get down. He'd——

Suddenly something shook the rope, nearly knocking him loose. Rawley's deep voice growled above him.

"You down there! You kid!"

Pete gulped. The rope shook again. Pete clung tight.

"Y–yes?" Pete said. "I'm here."

"Come back up."

"I'm going down," Pete said stubbornly.

"You'll go down all of a sudden!" growled the man. "I'll cut the rope if you don't come back up."

Pete looked down. The sidewalk was still thirty feet below him. If it had been deep grass, he might have risked the drop. But a cement sidewalk—he knew a couple of broken legs would be the least he'd get.

"Okay, kid." The voice came again. "I'll count three. Then I cut the rope."

"Wait a minute, wait a minute!" Pete shouted. "I'm coming. Give me time to get this rope tight around my hands. It's slipping."

"All right, but no tricks."

Pete had had an idea. It might not work, but it was the only thing he could think of. Hanging on by his left hand, he pulled his right glove off with his teeth. Then he reached in his pocket for his blue chalk.

Working swiftly, Pete made an enormous blue question mark, at least a yard high, on the dirty white face of the theater. It was the only clue he could leave. Then he dropped the chalk and jammed his glove back on.

"Okay, kid!" The voice above sounded impatient. "Come on up, or down you go!"

"I'm coming! I'm coming!"

Hand over hand, Pete struggled upward. As he got level with the opening in the minaret, strong hands reached out and dragged him in.

There were three men in the tower with Jupiter. Two of them were holding the First Investigator tightly. Jupiter looked scared and angry and indignant. Pete knew how he felt. He felt that way, too.

But what was it all about? First the gnomes, now these three men——

Pete started to ask a question. But Rawley interrupted him by shoving him forward.

"Get moving, kid," he said. "All right, Chuck, Driller, let's get these kids down into the cellar. We've got to get back to work and they can watch us."

The three men hustled Pete and Jupiter down the narrow stairs, then down some more stairs, until they found themselves in an extensive, concrete-lined cellar beside a couple of big, rusty boilers. Pete guessed they had once been used for heating the theater.

On one wall were several closed doors. In faded lettering, they said, "Coal Bin No. 1," "Coal Bin No. 2" and

"Coal Bin No. 3."

Rawley opened the door to Coal Bin No. 1, and pushed them inside.

Pete gave a grunt of astonishment. The four little men were sitting in a far corner playing cards. They showed little interest in the boys now, barely glancing up from their game. Several wheelbarrows, pickaxes and shovels and some large electric lanterns were strewn on the floor. But what surprised Pete most was a hole in the concrete wall, which must be the foundation of the theater. Through it he could see a long dark tunnel.

Pete figured rapidly. The direction the tunnel was going would lead it to Miss Agawam's house. No, it would go underneath Miss Agawam's house to something beyond it.

And then at last Pete realized what Jupe had meant by saying the nearest treasure was in the bank.

The three men, and the strange little creatures assisting them, were bank robbers. He and Jupe had stumbled on a brilliantly daring bank robbery!

Chapter Thirteen

A Sinister Plot Is Revealed

Pete and Jupiter sat on a pile of burlap sacks, leaning back against a concrete wall. Their hands and feet were tied, but they could talk. Except that Jupe didn't seem to feel much like talking.

Pete could see that he was annoyed at himself for not having figured out in the beginning what was happening. But how could you figure you were butting in on a bank robbery when you were only looking for some gnomes reported by an elderly lady who might actually be imagining them?

While he sat there, Pete had been working the whole thing out.

In the first place, Rawley was obviously in charge. The other two men took orders from him—the short, stocky one named Chuck and the small, wiry one called Driller. Driller had a thin mustache and a gold front tooth, and looked at the boys in a very ominous manner.

"Jupe," Pete whispered, "Rawley is really a bank robber, isn't he? He got the job as night watchman here so he could have a chance to rob the Third Merchants' Bank."

"That's it, Pete," Jupiter answered in a low voice. "I

should have guessed something like this from the beginning. I had two essential facts. A bank on the corner—and someone digging very close to it. That should have told me all I needed to know. And instead I let myself be distracted by thoughts of gnomes."

"Even Sherlock Holmes might not have thought of it," Pete told him. "Those gnomes sure kept us from thinking of a bank robbery. But one thing I don't figure, Jupe—why are the gnomes just sitting around and not helping?"

"Because they aren't really part of the gang," Jupiter muttered, still sounding gloomy. "Obviously they were hired to frighten Miss Agawam and keep people from taking any talk of digging seriously."

"Oh." Pete pondered this. "I get it—I think. But how did Mr. Rawley get hold of the gnomes? Did they come all the way from the Black Forest?"

"Pete," Jupiter sighed, "I'm disappointed in you. Those gnomes never saw the Black Forest. They came straight out of those children's books Miss Agawam used to write. I deduced that as soon as I saw them in the yard."

He seemed to expect Pete to understand him, so Pete chewed on the statement for a while. The gnomes came out of Miss Agawam's books? It might be simple to Jupe, but Pete just couldn't figure it.

Meanwhile, preparations for the bank robbery were going ahead. The three men were busy digging at the other end of the tunnel, hauling the loose dirt out in wheelbarrows. They dumped it outside, apparently into one of the other empty coal bins. Then they went back for another load.

"Only ten feet more, Driller!" Pete heard Chuck say as the two men passed in front of the boys.

"Then I can get to work with my tools, eh?" Driller said and rubbed his hands. "I'll drill into that concrete vault like a dentist going into a tooth."

They kept on working, extending the tunnel the last few feet to the waiting bank vault. Meanwhile, the little men just took it easy, their share of the work done.

Another question occurred to Pete. He turned to Jupiter.

"Jupe——" he began. Then he stopped. Jupe was stretched out on the burlap bags, asleep!

Pete almost woke him up. What business did the First Investigator have going to sleep at a time like this? They needed his brains to get them out of this mess!

Then Pete realized that they had a long night ahead of them. They would need their energy for the critical moment when the bank had been robbed and the gang started to leave. So Jupiter had done the most sensible thing he could think of. He'd gone to sleep.

Just thinking about it made Pete sleepy. After all, it was pretty late. And since there wasn't anything else he could do——

Pete fell asleep, too.

How long he slept Pete didn't know, but when he woke up he felt well rested. He was stiff, and his wrists and ankles hurt where they were tied, but his mind was alert again. He heard voices close to him.

He wriggled around and saw that Jupe was sitting up, holding a cup of soup in his tied hands. Mr. Rawley sat on a box beside Jupiter, looking in a very good humor.

The digging seemed to have stopped. The gnomes were sitting in a corner, eating sandwiches. Chuck and Driller were not in sight. Then Pete noticed a heavy electric cable snaking its way into the mouth of the tunnel. Very faintly he could hear grinding noises. That must be Driller, boring into the concrete side of the bank vault.

Jupiter noticed Pete sitting up and said, "Good morning, Pete. I hope you had a good sleep."

"Oh sure, fine and dandy," Pete grumbled, wriggling to get the stiffness out of his back. "The mattresses here are super. Can't be beat."

Mr. Rawley threw back his head and guffawed.

"You kids!" he said. "You give me a kick! I was pretty annoyed at you for butting in, but now that I have you safe and sound where you can't do any harm, no hard feelings."

"You had us fooled, all right," Jupiter told the man. "When I saw your gnomes playing games out in the yard, I thought Roger Agawam had hired them to scare his aunt. Then when I realized they had lured us into this old theater, it finally came to me what the plot had to be."

"You sure did," Rawley said. "A little more luck on your side and you'd have had the cops down on us by now."

He turned to Pete.

"You got a mighty smart partner here," he said. "Even if he looks sort of stupid most of the time. But that's good, that would help him in my business. People would never suspect him. If he'll throw in with me, I'll train him. In ten years he'll be the smartest criminal around."

"No thank you," Jupiter said politely. "A life of crime is hazardous and leads to ultimate disaster."

"Wow!" Rawley said. "Listen to that language. Kid, you could work right now with the biggest brains in the country. The idea is to plan everything ahead of time, like I did on this job. I'll live like a rich man for the rest of my life, and you—well, since you won't throw in with me I'd rather not say where you will be."

The words gave Pete a very crawly sensation.

"Pete has a lot of questions he'd like to ask," Jupiter said quickly. "Why don't you tell him how you came to figure out this bank robbery, Mr. Rawley?"

"Sure, kid," Rawley said. "Here, have a drink of soup."

He took the aluminum cup Jupe had been drinking from, filled it with hot soup from a vacuum bottle, and handed it to Pete.

"It's like this," Rawley said. "I was born and brought up right in the next block to this one. Forty years ago I was one of Miss Agawam's gnomes."

He chuckled. "Imagine me a gnome!" he said. "But that's what she called us. Once a week she'd have a party for all the kids around, and serve ice cream and cookies, and read us her books."

Mr. Rawley went on with his story. When he was a boy, his father, a construction worker, had actually helped build the Moorish Theater and the Third Merchants' Bank.

One day his father had happened to mention the bank's big underground vault. It had an enormous steel door, but the walls weren't steel at all—just concrete.

They had never been strengthened, because the vault was considered to be too far underground for any bank robbers to get to it.

"But me," Mr. Rawley said, "I've been thinking about what my dad said all these years. I figured that if somebody started in Miss Agawam's cellar, they could dig right up to that bank vault and drill in through the concrete side.

"But Miss Agawam never moved. When the theater shut down, I had a new idea. I figured a fellow could start digging from this building, dig right under Miss Agawam's house, and get to the bank vault with only a little more trouble.

"But then I got into some trouble with the law. As soon as I got out, I went to work on my scheme. I rounded up the gang I needed. Then I had to get into this theater. I scared away two night watchmen by making strange noises. Finally, Mr. Jordan hired me and I was ready to go."

Rawley related how he and Driller and Chuck had cut through the concrete wall, then begun tunneling directly beneath Miss Agawam's house. The dirt they excavated had been stored in the locked empty coal bins, so that even if the new owner, Mr. Jordan, had looked, he wouldn't have seen anything suspicious.

"So Mr. Jordan isn't in on this scheme?" Jupiter asked. "I thought he might be."

"No. I've played him for a sucker, just like I've played everyone else. Miss Agawam, for instance. I knew if she heard digging, she'd report it to the police. But Miss Agawam has this thing about believing in gnomes. So I brought around some gnomes to slip into her place at night and mess up her books and stuff. I had them dress up like those pictures in one of her books.

"I hoped to scare her into moving away. But suppose instead she reported to the police that gnomes were bothering her and digging under her house. Why, they might have taken her away to a hospital. Then I wouldn't have a thing to worry about."

Rawley rocked with laughter.

"As it is," he said, "she stayed scared, but she got hold of you kids. You were more of a nuisance. But luckily we were able to nab you in time."

"Suppose Miss Agawam's nephew Roger had believed her?" Jupiter asked. "Suppose he'd stayed in the house and heard digging, too? The police might have believed him."

Rawley winked at him with elaborate slowness.

"I said I played everyone for a sucker, didn't I? I got the job here from Jordan. I fooled Miss Agawam. Well, I made a deal with Roger."

"A deal?" Pete exclaimed.

"Sure. I told him that Jordan had hired me to make Roger's aunt a little nervous, so she would sell the property. I said I wasn't going to hurt her—just let her see some gnomes and hear some digging. Then she might sell out to Jordan in a hurry.

"Roger wanted her to sell and take the money while she could get it. So he agreed, as long as I promised not to hurt her. So naturally when she talked about gnomes and digging sounds he pretended he didn't believe a word of it."

Rawley looked pleased with himself.

"Golly, Jupe!" Pete said. "You were partly right about Roger, anyway. He was in on the scheme all along."

"You figured that?" Rawley asked Jupiter. "Kid, you're even smarter than I said. Throw in with me and we will stand the police of this country right on their heads. You have the brains for it."

"Well——" Jupiter looked thoughtful. Pete had an idea the notion of being a super-criminal rather attracted Jupiter. "Let me think about it a little more."

"Sure thing, kid. Well, I'm going to see if Driller and Chuck have bored through the cement wall into the vault yet."

As he turned to go, Pete stopped him with a question.

"I guess I understand the plot, and it's a pretty smart one," he said. "But where did you find the gnomes and how did you get them to cooperate?"

Rawley grinned. "They'll tell you," he said. He called to the group of little men. "Hey, Small Fry," he said. "Come here and talk to these two."

He disappeared into the tunnel. A gnome with fiery red eyes and dirty white beard came over and squatted on his heels, looking up at the boys.

"You boys gave us a lot of trouble," he said, in a high voice. "Nearly broke my arm, too. But I won't hold any grudges, because as soon as this is over you're going on a long sea voyage you won't come back from."

The little creature spoke good English, though with a certain European accent. Pete studied him in the dim light. The red eyes, the pointed ears, the big hairy hands, —he couldn't imagine how such a creature could have gone around unnoticed. Except maybe by living underground.

"Listen," Pete said. "Are you a real gnome? Or what are you, anyway?"

The little man sniggered.

"Boy, have we had you guessing!" he said. "Watch!"

Deliberately, he tugged at one hairy ear. Pete felt a moment of horror as the ear came loose from his head. Then he saw it was just a big, artificial ear that had been attached over a small, normal pink one.

Next the "gnome" pulled off a big hairy hand to reveal a tiny hand, smaller than a boy's. He pulled some false fangs out of his mouth. Finally, he carefully felt at one eye, twisted something loose and stared at Pete with a smirk.

"Look, kid, one red eye and no fangs!" he said. It was true that now he had only one red eye. The other was a normal blue.

"Tinted contact lenses," he said. He touched his nose. "Plastic nose," he said. "Artificial beard. Everything modeled right after those pictures in the old lady's books. I'm really a midget, kid, and if you call me a gnome again, I'll put a magic spell on you and turn you into a turnip."

He broke into shrill, high-pitched laughter. Jupiter gazed at Pete.

"Now, Pete, surely you understand everything," he said.

"I understand we've been made prize suckers by a bunch of midgets!" Pete said. "That much I understand. But if you mean do I understand just why they did it and everything—well, uh, there are a couple of teeny little things I'm not clear about."

"You do understand how Mr. Rawley made this plan to rob the Third Merchants' Bank by tunneling into the vault?" Jupiter asked. "And how he used the fake gnomes to keep Miss Agawam from telling anyone about the digging, with the cooperation of her nephew Roger?"

"Oh sure, all of that has finally penetrated," Pete said ruefully. "When did you dope it out, Jupe?"

"About the time I saw the midgets dart into the open door," Jupiter said. "Then it all came to me in one big flash. The bank—the digging—the gnomes—it all finally made sense."

"But it's too late," the midget said smugly. "You see, we only had to keep the old lady quiet, and things under control, until today. Today we grab the loot and make our getaway. And it's Sunday, so nobody will know what's happened until tomorrow."

"Miss Agawam will miss us," Jupiter said, trying to sound confident. "She'll call the police."

"She won't. She's already beat it in her nephew's car. Probably thinks you ran away or something. We have everything worked out like a breeze, kid. We'll have twenty-four hours before the bank even knows its been robbed."

Pete felt his heart drop. Jupiter started to say something, but at that moment Mr. Rawley emerged from the tunnel.

"Driller is through into the vault," he said. "We need some help getting the money out. A couple of you midgets come along to give us a hand."

"May I come, too?" Jupiter spoke up. "I'd like to watch your technique, Mr. Rawley."

"Sure, kid," the big man said. "I still hope you'll throw in with us when you see how smooth we operate."

He cut the rope around Jupe's feet, leaving his hands tied. Jupiter followed Rawley and three of the midgets into the tunnel, leaving Pete alone with the one he had been talking to.

"We sure made suckers out of you!" the midget snickered. "Standing on each other's shoulders to tap on the window and make sure you saw us. Doing acrobatics on the lawn until you chased us. Then leading you in through the door, so we had you trapped. I have to hand it to you, though. You came pretty close to making a getaway."

"Thanks for nothing," Pete replied. "But why did you need to catch us?"

"Because this is the big night, like I said. If you'd heard digging, your partner would have tumbled and called the cops. We had to get you out of the way until we lifted the loot and made our getaway."

Pete was puzzled. "But look," he said. "How can you hope to keep from being caught by the police? Midgets are easy to find. The police will come straight to you when we tell them our story."

"If you *could* tell them your story!" the little man retorted. "You won't be around to do any talking. But, supposing you did, and the police came after us. This is Hollywood, U.S.A., where they make all the movies, remember?"

"What of it?" Pete asked.

"Why, there are as many midgets in Hollywood as in the rest of the world put together. We're all hoping for jobs in the movies, or TV, or at Disneyland. About thirty of us live together in a special boarding house. Some of us have a little sideline—we sneak through transoms and open windows and lift stuff. Or we help out on a job like this one. Our size makes it easy for us to do things no ordinary man can.

"But us midgets are one big happy family, understand? None of us would tell on another. If anybody asks us, we don't know anything, didn't hear anything, and can't guess anything about any other midget."

"Besides," the tiny man went on, slipping on his artificial ear, "you can't identify any of us. Even if you ever get a chance to try. Which isn't very likely."

With that ominous remark, he got up and disappeared into the tunnel.

Jupiter meanwhile was standing in an enlarged space outside a concrete wall. A hole had been drilled through the concrete—a hole big enough for a small boy to get through. Chuck and Driller, weary from their labors, were mopping their foreheads.

"We could make the hole bigger," Chuck told Rawley. "But it would take time. The midgets can climb through and hand out the loot."

"Right." Rawley boosted the tiny men one by one through the neatly drilled hole. Inside, their flashlights illuminated a large square room. Cash and securities were neatly stacked on shelves. Sacks of silver coins lined the floor.

"Quarter of a million!" Rawley gloated. "Pay roll is

Monday—end of the month. Big airplane factory down the street banks here."

With keen interest Jupiter watched the midgets pass the bundles of cash and securities through the hole. The three men loaded them into burlap bags. Finally everything of value was taken, except the bags of coins.

"Leave the coins," Chuck suggested. "Too heavy. We have enough."

"Right," Rawley said. "No, hand out two sacks of coins."

With much huffing and puffing, the little men managed to push two heavy bags of silver through the hole. Then they climbed out.

When they had trundled everything in wheelbarrows back to the coal bin, Rawley cut open one bundle and handed a sheaf of bills to each midget.

"There you are, ten thousand dollars apiece," he said. "Be careful how you spend it. Now get out of those gnome outfits. We're almost ready to leave."

"Not any too soon," Driller muttered. "We're running behind schedule."

Rawley ignored him and turned to Jupiter.

"Well, kid?" he asked. "Now that you've seen how we operate, are you going to throw in with us? You'll be a rich man—you have the brains to make a big-time criminal."

Pete wondered what Jupiter would say. He couldn't believe Jupiter would agree, but ——

"I'd like to think about it a little more," Jupiter said. "After I have seen how you organize your getaway. After all, commission of a crime is only half the job. Getting away is equally important and it's where most criminals fall down."

Rawley laughed.

"I told you he had brains," he said to the others. "Okay, we'll take you with us on our getaway. Only you'll have to travel in disguise, sort of. Chuck—Driller —dress 'em up."

At that the two men suddenly pounced on the boys. They slid two large burlap sacks over their heads, down to their feet, where they tied the ends of the bags securely.

"We'll load 'em on the truck and take 'em with us," Rawley said. "Let's get busy."

Driller objected. The kids would be a nuisance. Why not just leave them where they were and . . . His voice dropped so Pete, inside the bag, couldn't hear the rest of what he said. But he heard Rawley laugh.

"No need for that," he said. "Why do you think I took those two bags of silver? Any time we want to get rid of them we just tie the bags around their feet and drop them over the side of the ship.

"They'll be the two richest kids in Davy Jones's Locker!"

Chapter Fourteen

Bob Hunts for His Friends

Bob Andrews woke slowly to Sunday morning sunshine pouring in his window. For a moment he lay still, lazily enjoying that moment when you aren't quite awake and have nothing on your mind.

Then a thought hit him like a bumblebee sting and he leaped out of bed. Jupiter and Pete! What had happened during the night? Had they discovered anything? Had they left a message?

He slipped into his clothes. Automatically pushing his walkie-talkie into a pocket, he went downstairs. His mother was cooking pancakes in the kitchen, and the aroma of maple syrup tickled his nose.

"Any message from Jupiter, Mom?" Bob asked.

"No, he hasn't phoned anything about Green Gate One or Purple Gate Eight or anything like that. So you can just sit down and eat these nice pancakes I've fixed, and not hurry over to that junk yard."

"It's a salvage yard, Mom, and we don't have any Purple Gate Eight," Bob corrected, loading a plate with pancakes.

As long as Jupiter hadn't phoned, things must be all

110

right. Maybe they had had a quiet night and were still asleep. Or maybe they had left a message at the salvage yard.

He ate without hurrying, and then biked over to The Jones Salvage Yard. The main gate was open and Hans was in the yard washing the small truck.

"Any phone call from Jupe?" Bob asked.

"No call, all is quiet I guess," Hans said.

"He ought to be up by now." Bob's forehead furrowed. "I better call, then we'll go down and get him. We're going to take more lessons in scuba diving today."

He entered the little office and dialed Miss Agatha Agawam's number. It rang and rang but, to his amazement, there was no answer. He tried again. Still no answer. Bob began to feel the first sensations of alarm.

"They don't answer," he told Hans. "Where could they be? I mean, Miss Agawam ought to be home. If she's gone, too——"

Hans looked suddenly very serious.

"They went to catch gnomes. I think gnomes have caught them!" he said grimly.

"We'd better go down and see what's happening," Bob said. "Let's get there as fast as we can."

"You bet your shoes!" Hans said.

At that moment the telephone rang loudly.

"Maybe that's Jupiter now!" Bob cried. He raced inside and scooped up the phone.

"Hello?" he said. "Jones Salvage Yard."

"Excuse, please, is Jupiter-san present?" asked a boy's voice, and Bob recognized it as Taro Togati.

"No, he's out on a case. This is Bob Andrews."

"Please give Jupiter-san message. Message is this. My father and guards search museum all last night for Golden Belt. They look behind pictures and in every place possible."

"And they found it?" Bob asked excitedly.

"Alas, no. They found nothing. My father is again angry at himself for listening to the foolishness of boys. I am in disgrace, too. But I still think it a very good idea Jupiter-san had. Tell him, though, belt was not found."

"I'll tell him when I see him," Bob said. He hung up and went out and climbed in the truck. This news would really make Jupiter gloomy. Well, it *had* been a good idea that the belt was hidden in the museum all along. Jupe wasn't wrong often, but this time it certainly seemed he had been.

They started downtown with a roar. Traffic on the Los Angeles freeways was lighter than usual, and they made such speed that the old truck rattled and groaned. Forty-five minutes later they pulled up outside of Miss Agatha Agawam's old house in the downtown district.

Before the motor stopped, Bob had hopped out of the truck and was ringing the bell.

He pressed a long time, without getting an answer.

By now Bob was very much alarmed.

He called to Hans. As Hans climbed out of the truck, Bob noticed that the gate was not quite shut. He pushed it open, and he and Hans hurried up on the porch.

They rang the doorbell long and loudly. Silence answered them.

"Try the door," Hans suggested. "Maybe they are inside turned to rocks."

Hans couldn't seem to get over the idea that the gnomes had turned Pete and Jupe into rocks. But Bob tried the door. To his surprise it opened. He called out several times.

Only a faint echo of his own voice replied.

Desperate with anxiety, Bob and Hans searched the whole house, including the cellar. There was no trace anywhere of Pete and Jupiter. Or of Miss Agawam either. The only things they found were the zipper bags and the open leather kit in the room upstairs.

"Jupe and Pete saw something and they went to investigate!" Bob said, thinking swiftly now. "Maybe Miss Agawam followed them and got caught, too! We have to look for them!"

"Gnomes have caught them all," Hans said. He sounded very gloomy. It was obvious Hans had a great respect for gnomes and their powers.

"We have to look!" Bob said worriedly. He didn't actually believe Pete and Jupe had been turned into rocks, but on the other hand, something pretty serious must have happened to them. "First we search the outside yard."

They searched the outside yard without finding a clue until Bob saw Jupiter's camera dangling from a bush at the corner of the house. He pounced on it.

"Jupe was out here!" he said. "He took a picture of something. Let's see what he photographed!"

It took only seconds to pull the developed picture out. But when they saw it they both gulped.

It was a picture of a wild-eyed gnome, with hairy ears and fanglike front teeth, peering in a window!

"Wow!" Hans said. "What did I tell you, Bob? Gnomes have got Pete and Jupe for sure."

"Maybe," Bob said, not knowing what to think now. "Just the same we have to hunt for them. We'll get the police and ——"

But the thought of showing that picture to the police made him hesitate. No, he and Hans would look first, he decided.

"Listen, Hans," Bob said swiftly. "They aren't in the house or the yard. But they went out last night to catch something and didn't come back. Maybe they left a clue, or maybe someone saw them. First we'll go all around this block. Then the next. We'll ask anyone we see if they saw or heard anything in the night."

Bob led the way to the street. The theater end was closest so he started that way. The street was quiet, and they didn't see any people around to ask nor any signs of a clue. As they came opposite the front of the Moorish Theater, Bob stepped on something that crunched under his shoe.

He looked down. Then he gave a yell. He had stepped on a piece of broken blue chalk.

"Pete's special chalk!" he told Hans. "Pete was around here somewhere last night."

"Look here!" Hans said. Close to the wall lay the other half of the broken blue chalk.

"It was all one piece and it broke," Bob said. "Hans, look at this. See? There is a mark on the sidewalk where it fell and broke!"

"Fall? Where did it fall from?" Hans asked.

But already Bob was backing away, staring upward.

No open windows, no places where a boy Pete's size might be hiding——

Then he saw it. It was almost invisible, because of the dirt that had accumulated on the white front of the theater. But it was there:

?

An enormous question mark in blue chalk. Pete's special sign!

It meant that somehow, sometime last night Pete had been halfway up the front wall of the closed theater!

For the life of him, Bob couldn't figure out how this was possible, but the mark meant a lot just the same. It meant that there was a chance Pete and Jupiter might be inside now.

"Hans, we have to get inside the theater!" Bob said tensely.

"Okay, I will pull boards off and break in the door," Hans said. He started to pull loose the boards that sealed up the main entrance. But Bob stopped him.

"If they're inside, there's probably a door open," he said. "I think I know where it is."

He led Hans around the building and almost to the alley that ran behind the theater and Miss Agawam's house.

"Shhh!" he said. "Now we have to take security measures."

From the breast pocket of his jacket he took a small round mirror. It was a piece of new equipment Jupe had issued to The Three Investigators just that week.

Bob lay down on his stomach on the sidewalk and

wriggled up to the corner where the alley began. Very cautiously he thrust the mirror out beyond the corner and angled it so he could see the length of the alley.

There was something there. A green panel truck stood just outside the stage door where he and the others had been the day before!

Bob watched in the mirror with growing excitement. He was surprised to see a big man come out of the theater, lugging a large, heavy canvas sack. It was Mr. Rawley.

"Bob, you see something?" Hans asked.

"I see the night watchman doing something mighty peculiar. I think he's stealing something," Bob whispered, still flat on the sidewalk. "Anyway, I'm positive Pete and Jupiter are inside."

"Well, what do we wait for? We will go get them." Hans flexed his powerful muscles.

"No, we need the police. There might be a whole lot of them in there—yes, here come two more men carrying burlap bags. Find some policemen and hurry back, Hans. I'll stay on watch."

"Okay," Hans grumbled, obviously sure he could do a better job by himself. He hurried away. Bob kept watch.

From time to time the men glanced sharply up and down the alley. But they did not notice the small mirror held just above the pavement. The three—one thin and wiry, one short and squat, and the big, heavy-set Mr. Rawley—continued carrying out burlap sacks and stowing them in the truck.

Bob began to fidget. Time was running out. Why didn't Hans come back with a policeman?

Now the three men seemed to have finished loading the truck. They held a brief consultation. Then they went back inside and this time two of them emerged with a bigger burlap sack.

The burlap sack wriggled! It tried to tear itself loose.

The men shoved it into the truck and went back for a similar sack, even stouter and heavier. This one also wriggled as it went into the truck.

Bob felt frustrated. He was positive Pete and Jupiter were in those last two sacks, and he couldn't do a thing to help them. If Hans had been there, they could have rushed the men and possibly freed his friends. But he'd sent Hans away to find a policeman. And Bob knew that if he tried to help by himself, he'd just be caught, too.

One of the men swung the rear door of the truck shut. All three got in the front seat. An instant later it was moving away down the alley.

Jupiter and Pete were in it and he'd lost his chance to rescue them!

Chapter Fifteen

The Trail Is Lost

Jupiter and Pete were very uncomfortable. Hands and feet tied, burlap sacks scratching their faces, they lay on bundles of money and securities stolen from the Third Merchants' Bank.

Pete could feel Jupe moving beside him. Jupe was testing his bonds.

"Jupe," Pete whispered through the sack. "Where do you think they are taking us?"

"A ship was mentioned," Jupe whispered back. "Probably they are going to flee by water."

"Did you hear what Mr. Rawley said about tying sacks of silver coins to our feet and dropping us overboard?"

"I heard," Jupiter answered. "However, remember that the famous magician, Harry Houdini, used to let himself be manacled with handcuffs, sealed in a milk can, and tossed into the water. He always came out alive."

"That would make me feel a lot better if I was Harry Houdini," Pete growled. "But I'm Pete Crenshaw and I haven't had any practice. I don't want to be the richest kid in Davy Jones's locker."

They were interrupted by a giggle. The four midgets had put on the clothing of small boys and were riding in the back of the truck with the two captives. Now one of them spoke.

"Maybe you'll be lucky," he said in his high, childlike voice. "Maybe Mr. Rawley will sell you for slaves somewhere in Asia. They still have slaves way back in the deserts of Arabia."

Pete was silent, mulling this over. Did he want to be a slave to some faraway Arabian sheik? Or would he rather be the main course for a school of fish? Neither alternative appealed to him in the slightest.

Now the midgets were silent. The truck full of stolen money jolted along. Then it slowed for a moment.

"All right, Small Fry, hop out and catch your bus!" came Rawley's booming voice from up front. "You've been paid. Remember, don't let anyone see you spending the money for a long time."

"We'll hide it, don't worry," one midget promised.

"And don't talk! Keep your lips buttoned!" snapped Chuck.

"We never talk to police," said the midget. "Us midgets stick together. They'll go crazy trying to pin anything on us."

With that the truck slowed still more, the rear door opened, and one by one the midgets hopped out. The door slammed shut. The truck picked up speed. In a moment it went up a slope and turned onto a smoother road. Its speed increased. Obviously they were now on a freeway, probably leading to the shore of the Pacific Ocean, a few miles away. There, no doubt, a ship was waiting for the bank robbers.

"A slave, or a meal for fish," Pete groaned. "Jupe, we're done for. Why did we ever start this investigation business anyway?"

"For excitement," Jupiter answered, his voice muffled. "And to use our wits."

"I've had enough excitement for a thousand years, and my wits are frozen solid," Pete complained. "The bank robbers have gotten away free and clear. I did hope Bob would see the only clue I could leave, but it was a pretty far-fetched hope. Well, say something!" he urged, irritated by his friend's silence. "At least tell me we have a chance!"

"I can't," Jupiter said honestly. "I was just thinking that Mr. Rawley has really been very clever."

At that moment, a car's length behind, Bob Andrews and Hans were grimly following them.

Hans had returned, unable to find a policeman anywhere, just as Bob saw the green truck drive down the alley. Bob started to tell Hans he should have found a telephone and called the police. Then he realized that in such a quiet neighborhood, with everything closed for Sunday, a telephone was probably as unlikely to be found as a policeman.

So he grabbed Hans and led him to the waiting salvage-yard truck. They hopped in and started off.

The green truck had a blue rear door, apparently a replacement after an accident, making it easy to follow. Sunday morning traffic was light, and there was nothing about the salvage yard's ramshackle old truck to arouse suspicion.

"Don't lose them, Hans!" Bob urged. "Pete and Jupiter are in that truck!"

"I could ram it," Hans said hopefully. "Knock it off the road. That would stop it for sure."

"And maybe kill Jupe and Pete!" Bob said. "You know that wouldn't work. Follow it until it stops."

So they drove slowly along, following the truck. After five minutes it slowed down and they hoped it would stop. Instead, the rear door opened and four small boys hopped out and marched to a bus stop.

"By Jiminy!" Hans muttered grimly. "Little boys up to mischief. What shall I do, Bob? Grab them, and make them talk?"

"No, no!" Bob replied. "Then we'll lose the truck."

An instant later the green truck pulled onto a freeway and started roaring west, in the direction of the ocean.

Startled, Hans just barely got onto the freeway in time to avoid losing them. Now, the truck ahead was going so fast that Hans could hardly keep up.

"I wonder if Jupe or Pete can use their walkie-talkies," Bob said, remembering a previous occasion when these devices had come in handy. "I'll listen in and see."

He tugged his walkie-talkie from his pocket, pushed the *On* button, and held it to his ear. For a moment he just heard humming.

Then to his surprise he made out a man's voice, very loud, which he recognized as Rawley's. Apparently Rawley was using a powerful walkie-talkie, operating on the Citizens' Band like Bob's.

"Hello, Harbor!" he was saying. "Hello, Harbor! This

is Operation Tunnel calling. Can you read me? Come in. Come in."

Bob listened intently. In a moment a fainter voice answered.

"Hello, Operation Tunnel. This is Harbor, standing by. Did Operation Tunnel go off successfully?"

"Hello Harbor!" That was Rawley's voice again. "Couldn't be smoother. Except that we picked up a couple of passengers. We can decide what to do with them when we get aboard. That is all. Will broadcast again when we reach dock. Over and out."

With that the walkie-talkie went dead.

Immediately there was a loud bang. Bob ducked. The men ahead must have seen them and fired at them!

The salvage-yard truck was wobbling. Hans steered it onto the safety strip alongside the road.

"We go too fast," he said. "Bob, we have a blowout. We must stop."

An instant later the green truck with the blue door, carrying Pete and Jupiter, had disappeared into the distance.

Chapter Sixteen

Desperate Chances

Hans put on the spare tire as swiftly as he could. But it took at least ten minutes and by then, of course, the green truck was miles away.

They had lost Jupiter and Pete. Bob had a funny sinking feeling he would never see them again.

"What do we do now, Bob?" Hans asked when they were back in the front seat. "Go for the police?"

"I forgot to write down the license number of that truck," Bob confessed, feeling very sheepish. "We were so busy following it. There's nothing much we could tell the police."

"Well, they go this way, so we must go this way," Hans said. He let in the gears and the truck moved back onto the freeway, headed west.

Bob was thinking furiously. The road they were on led to the Pacific Ocean. One branch, farther on, would take them to the charming seaside town of Long Beach. Another branch would take them to San Pedro Harbor, the official shipping port for the city of Los Angeles.

On the walkie-talkie the voice had mentioned a harbor. Long Beach wasn't a harbor. San Pedro was.

And it was the only one in that direction.

"Hans, head for San Pedro," he directed.

"Okay, Bob," Hans agreed.

They continued roaring along at the greatest speed the old truck was capable of. Bob meanwhile was wracking his brains trying to figure out what could have happened.

Pete and Jupiter had set out to watch for gnomes. They had wound up in burlap sacks in a truck driven by Mr. Rawley, the night watchman of the Moorish Theater. The strange series of events which had caused all this was impossible to imagine.

He only knew that his friends were in serious trouble and there was no one who could rescue them except himself. The thought made him feel extremely helpless.

Presently they came into the outskirts of San Pedro, its fields dotted by great derricks pumping up oil from far underground. They drove quickly through town to the harbor. It was not a very scenic spot, being mostly man-made, but it was crowded with freighters at the piers and at anchor in the dingy gray water.

Some fishing boats were also anchored in the harbor, and a few small craft were moving back and forth.

Hans stopped the truck and they both stared helplessly about.

Pete and Jupiter were destined for one of those ships, or maybe one of those fishing boats. They'd be taken aboard and never come back. If only there was some way to know which ship it was!

"I guess we are licked, Bob," Hans said. "There is no way to find that truck now. I look in every street and do not see it."

"It's at some pier," Bob said. "The walkie-talkie told us that much. But there are a lot of piers in San Pedro. By the time we examined them all——" Then he jumped as if stung.

"The walkie-talkie!" he said. "We heard them say they'd communicate again when they got here!"

He was in such a hurry it took him an extra couple of seconds to get the little instrument turned on. At first he heard nothing. Breathing hard, he held it close to his ear. Then a voice spoke.

"Operation Tunnel!" it said. "We have lowered boat and will pick you up at Pier 37 in five minutes. Have all luggage including passengers ready for immediate loading."

"This is Operation Tunnel," answered Rawley's voice. "We have you in sight. All luggage and passengers are waiting in truck, ready for loading."

"Very good," said the other voice. "No more communication. As we approach, wave a white handkerchief three times to indicate all is clear. Over and out."

The voices ended. But Bob was quivering with excitement.

"The truck is at Pier 37," he told Hans. "We have just five minutes, that's all. Where's Pier 37?"

"I do not know," Hans admitted. "I am not acquainted with San Pedro."

"We have to find someone to ask!" Bob panted. "A police officer if we can find one. Start up, Hans, and keep a sharp eye."

Hans started the truck and they moved slowly down the street, looking for someone to ask directions of. But it was Sunday morning and pedestrians were remarkably few. Then they saw a police patrol car turn into the street ahead of them.

"Pull up beside that car, Hans!" Bob yelled. "Honk like anything!"

Hans gunned the motor. The old truck rumbled up alongside the sleek little police car, its horn going *grrr-waaaah*! *grr-waaah*!

"Please, officer!" Bob yelled. "Where is Pier 37? It's a matter of life and death!"

"Pier 37?" The officer at the wheel pointed behind them. "Three blocks that way, then down the street toward the harbor. No, that's a one-way street. Go four blocks, turn down to the harbor, come back a block and——"

"Thanks!" Bob shouted. "Follow us! Two boys are in terrible danger!"

The truck roared away, leaving the officer still speaking. He blinked as the truck made a U-turn in the middle of the street, practically on two wheels, and roared away.

"Hey! That's illegal!" the officer said to his partner. Then he started the car, made a U-turn also and raced after them.

Hans sped down three blocks.

"Turn here!" Bob yelled. "It's a one-way street, but it's the quickest way, and our time is almost up!"

A small sign said "Pier 37," and an arrow pointed down the street. They went a block, then with a groan of dismay Hans brought the truck to a squealing stop.

Pier 37 was ahead of them, all right. But the entrance to it was blocked by a heavy iron-and-wire gate. The gate was padlocked.

Beyond it they could see the green truck with the blue door. A heavy-set man leaned against the front fender, casually waving a white handkerchief. Only a hundred yards out in the water a dilapidated motor launch was churning toward the pier.

"We are locked out, Bob!" Hans said. "They have Pete and Jupe for sure!"

At that moment the police car roared up beside them.

"You're under arrest!" shouted the officer at the wheel. "You made a U-turn, you were speeding, and you went down a one-way street the wrong way! Let me see your license."

"We have no time!" Hans yelled. "We must get out on Pier 37 quick!"

"They're not loading today," the other officer said. "And you've broken the law. Now let's see your license."

"Officer, you don't understand! The men in that truck are kidnapping two boys!" Bob yelled, poking his head around Hans. "Please help us stop them!"

"Fancy stories won't help you get out of this one!" the officer growled. "Now, mister, let me see your license."

With every second that passed, the launch drew closer to the pier.

"Hans!" Bob shouted with a sudden inspiration. "Drive fast! Break the gate down!"

"Okay, Bob, good idea!" Hans grunted. He stepped hard on the gas pedal and the truck shot ahead, leaving the policemen shouting after them.

As the big bumpers hit the middle of the locked gate, there was a noise like a shrill scream. Then gate and fence collapsed. The truck went forward a few feet, then the wire of the fence wrapped around the wheels, and it stalled, still fifty feet from the green truck.

"Come on, Bob!" Hans roared. He leaped out and dashed forward, Bob at his heels.

Hans bore down on Rawley like a runaway bull. Startled, Rawley saw him coming, and reached for something in his pocket, probably a gun. But before he could get it out, Hans had wrapped powerful arms around him, picked him up like a child and thrown him into the harbor. Rawley went under and came up sputtering. The oncoming launch stopped, and the men on it hauled him aboard.

Now Chuck and Driller, armed with a wrench and tire iron, jumped down from the truck, and rushed at Hans. Hans deftly ducked their blows, spun them around, and caught each by the collar. He marched them to the edge of the pier and into the water.

Meanwhile, Bob was busy at the rear door of the truck. He got it open and yelled inside, "Pete! Jupe! Is that you?"

"Bob!" It was Jupiter's muffled voice. "Get us out of these bags!"

"Rah for Bob!" said Pete, more faintly because Jupiter was partly lying on him.

Meanwhile, the launch picked up Chuck and Driller and turned at high speed, heading for a fishing boat out in the harbor.

Having seen Hans's strength, the two police officers approached him cautiously, waving revolvers.

"You're under arrest!" one of them shouted. "I don't

know how many laws you've broken, but it's plenty, I know that."

"Ha!" Hans snorted. He pointed to the departing launch. "You catch that boat. Then you have the right fellows."

Unnoticed, Bob was busy with his knife, cutting the burlap bags off Jupiter and Pete, then freeing their hands and feet. The two boys stood up and stretched, looking very tousled. They blinked their eyes while getting used to the light.

The second police officer noticed the boys emerging from the sacks, and he came over looking puzzled.

"Say, what's going on here, anyway?" he asked. "What were you kids doing in those sacks? Is this some kind of stunt?"

Jupiter drew himself up and mustered all of his dignity. He reached inside the truck for a burlap sack and, taking Bob's knife, cut a slit in it. Bundles of bills tumbled out on the pier. Then he took out one of The Three Investigators' business cards. He handed it to the officer.

"The Three Investigators have just finished solving a bad case of gnomes," he said in a grand manner. "They have also saved the loot from a daring bank robbery. The men who committed it are now trying to escape," he told the flabbergasted officers, "so we are turning the case over to the proper authorities. I think that covers everything."

Pete and Bob and Hans gazed at him in admiration. They had never seen Jupe look more impressive.

When it came to being dignified, you couldn't beat **Jupiter Jones!**

Chapter Seventeen

Surprise Attack

Six days had passed since that exciting Sunday. After Jupiter had said, "I think that covers everything," the boys had had to answer about a million questions.

Eventually the police agreed that they had indeed successfully prevented the thieves from getting away with the loot from the Third Merchants' Bank. They were skeptical at first about the part involving the "gnomes," but were finally convinced when Miss Agawam came forth to back up their story.

However, the police did not succeed in capturing the criminals. Rawley, Chuck and Driller got away by boat in a light fog that sprang up while the police were still questioning The Three Investigators. As for the midgets who impersonated gnomes, the wily little men simply denied everything. The police went to the theatrical boarding house where most midgets stayed in Hollywood. Every one of them had several friends who swore he hadn't been out of the house during the time of the bank robbery. No one could shake their stories, and it was impossible to make any arrests.

During most of the six days that had passed, Jupiter

had moped and acted grumpy. The fact is, he was angry at himself.

While it was true Jupe had finally deduced that the gnomes were disguised midgets, and then had guessed a bank robbery was in progress, he had done so only moments before he had been captured.

It was Pete who had left the clue on the outside wall of the theater. It was Bob who had found the clue. It was Bob and Hans who had saved Jupiter and Pete.

The truth was that Jupiter Jones, First Investigator, had not shone brightly in the case of Miss Agawam's "gnomes," or at least he didn't think so. And just to make things worse, his solution of the disappearance of the Golden Belt had also been wrong, in spite of his excellent logic. For Jupiter, this was a hard pill to swallow. Even the warm praise Miss Agawam had given them all only softened Jupiter's mood a little.

Something had to happen to get Jupiter back to feeling his normal self, and Bob and Pete hoped it would happen soon.

The following Saturday afternoon, after the three boys had put in a hard morning rebuilding some damaged junk, Bob, Pete and Jupe were taking it easy in the hidden workshop section of the salvage yard. Hard work with his hands had helped make Jupe a bit more cheerful, and he and Pete were filling in added details for Bob of their adventures in the old Moorish Theater.

"I'm surprised the police haven't located Rawley, or at least that fellow Driller by now," Pete commented. "Sooner or later Interpol will spot him. After all, that gold tooth of Driller's should make him pretty conspicuous."

"Lots of people have gold teeth," Bob said. "Even a little Cub Scout I bumped into at the museum had a gold tooth. Why, Jupe, what's the matter?"

Jupiter was acting very strangely. He had leaped to his feet and was staring at Bob as if he had never seen him before.

"You saw a little Cub Scout with a gold tooth?" he asked, his face pink with excitement. He leaned over and beat his fists on their printing press. "Bob!" he groaned. "Why didn't you tell me at the time? *Why didn't you tell me?!*"

"About seeing a Cub Scout with a gold tooth?" Bob asked, rather startled by Jupiter's actions. "I didn't think it was important . . . and I never thought of it again until right now."

"But don't you realize?" Jupiter said. "If you had told me, I could have——"

At that moment Mrs. Jones's powerful voice interrupted them, announcing a vistor. It turned out to be the Japanese boy, Taro Togati, looking very downcast.

"Jupiter-san," he said, making a little bow. "Bob-san. Pete-san. I come to say good-bye. My father is in disgrace. We return to Japan."

"What's the matter, Taro?" Jupiter asked. "Is the exhibition of the jewels being abandoned?"

"Ah, no." The small Japanese boy shook his head. "But you know the Golden Belt has never been found. It was not, alas, inside the museum as you so cleverly suggested. The guards have been proven innocent. And no new suspects were found. So the Nagasami Jewelry

Company dismisses my father as chief detective. He is much disgraced. He is as a man half dead."

The boys were sorry to hear this news. They liked little Taro. They knew his father had done the best he could—the gang that had robbed the Peterson Museum was just too smart.

However, Jupe was acting peculiarly. He was pinching his lower lip, setting his mental machinery in motion. His eyes were bright. All of his gloominess of the past week seemed gone.

"Taro!" he said. "Tomorrow is the last day of the exhibit, right?"

"Ah, so," Taro nodded. "Sunday night it closes. Sunday night my honorable father and I fly back to Japan. So I come today to say good-bye to my only American friends."

"Didn't I read in the paper," Jupiter asked, "that tomorrow is going to be Children's Day? All children under twelve admitted free, the rest at half fare?"

"Yes," agreed Taro. "Last time it was, what you call, big bust. So they decide to have another Children's Day."

"Then we have no time to lose! Taro, I have an idea. Will your father give me some cooperation?"

"Cooperation?" Taro did not quite grasp the word.

"Will he work with me on my idea?"

"Oh, yes!" Taro bobbed his head vigorously. "My father desperate. He say police not solve case, he willing to try boys now."

"Then let's go!" Jupe leaped up. "You have a car?"

"My father send me in car with driver."

"Good. Bob, Pete—you wait for us. I may be gone all

afternoon. Bob, keep writing up your notes so we can give this case to Mr. Hitchcock to read. Pete, keep on rubbing down that rusty power mower. We'll make ten dollars out of that. Get permission to stay here all night, if necessary."

With that, leaving Bob and Pete with their mouths hanging open, Jupiter was gone, tugging Taro Togati behind him.

It took Bob and Pete a minute to recover their voices.

"Well!" Pete said. "What was that all about?"

"Darned if I know," Bob answered. "All of a sudden something seemed to bite Jupe. I guess all we can do is wait until he gets back."

The mystery became greater when they received a telephone call from Jupiter in the latter part of the afternoon.

"Test all secret entrances and exits, except Emergency One and Secret Four," he ordered, referring to their escape and entry routes for use only under the most desperate conditions. "Use Green Gate One, Tunnel Two, Red Gate Rover, and Easy Three. Go in and out several times. Make sure they are all working smoothly."

That was all he would say. He hung up before they could ask questions.

What Jupiter had in mind was certainly beyond Pete and Bob. But they obeyed. They went in through Green Gate One—two boards of the fence painted green—and crawled in through the corrugated pipe of Tunnel Two.

Next they tried Red Gate Rover. This one consisted of three boards painted red as part of a scene of the San Francisco fire of 1906. A little dog sat watching the fire, and by pressing his eye they made the boards swing up. Once through, they crawled around and between and under junk stacked with seeming carelessness, until they reached the side of Headquarters. Here a panel admitted them.

Easy Three was the simplest entrance. A big oak door, still on its hinges, leaned against some timber in the yard. A big rusty key, concealed in a barrel of other rusty metal, opened the door. Behind it, a short passageway led to the original side door of the mobile home trailer that had been turned into Headquarters. Easy Three was used only when the yard was deserted and no one was looking.

Neither Bob nor Pete was happy about following Jupe's instructions, but he was head of the firm and they did what he said. They tested each entrance three times. Then they waited some more.

It was not until Mrs. Jones had held up supper almost an hour that Jupiter returned, looking hot but triumphant. Surprisingly he came in a taxicab. The cab drew up directly in front of the Jones's cottage and Jupe got out and paid the driver with a flourish. Bob and Pete were startled to see the cab then stop around the corner and little Taro creep up and scuttle into the house by the back door.

"Mercy and goodness and sweetness and light!" Mrs. Jones exclaimed as Jupiter came in. "What in the world are you up to now, Jupiter? You're wearing your best jacket and it will hardly button around your waist. You're positively fat."

Being called fat was one thing Jupiter disliked. He didn't mind being called stocky or muscular, but fat—no.

However, now he just grinned.

"If you're getting mixed up in another bank robbery, Jupiter my boy," said Mr. Jones, a small man with a large black mustache, who liked to talk in flowing English, "let me say that I am unalterably opposed. In other words, I disapprove. To put the matter simply, I forbid it."

"I'm just trying to help out Taro here," Jupiter said, putting a hand on the Japanese boy's shoulder. "His father is in a little trouble. He's misplaced a belt and I want to help him find it."

"Hmm." Mr. Jones thought about the remark until he finished serving the roast beef and mashed potatoes. "Misplaced a belt. I have turned that remark over in my mind several times and I can find no sinister aspects to it, so you may proceed."

The rest of the meal went swiftly. Jupiter and Taro both seemed distracted, and Jupiter didn't give Pete and Bob any clues as to what was in his mind. Also, he kept his jacket tightly buttoned, though it was a hot evening.

As the sky started to darken, Jupiter got up.

"If you'll excuse us, Aunt Mathilda and Uncle Titus," he said, "we're going to have a meeting in the yard."

"Oh yes, your club," his aunt said vaguely. She still clung to her original notion that the investigation firm was a club. "Go right ahead, boys, Titus and I will do the dishes."

"I hope you can help this lad's father find his lost belt," Titus Jones said, putting his hand on Taro's shoulder. "Well, run along."

"Er—for special reasons," Jupiter said," we don't want

anyone to know we have a guest. So I'm going to get Hans and Konrad to carry Taro over in a cardboard box."

This seemed peculiar to Bob and Pete, but Mr. and Mrs. Jones merely nodded. They were used to the odd things Jupiter sometimes did.

So presently Bob, Pete and Jupiter, followed by Hans and Konrad carrying a large box, assembled in the workshop area inside the yard. The men put the box down, and Taro crawled out.

As soon as the two yard helpers had left, Jupiter led the three boys into Headquarters through Tunnel Two.

Once they were all inside, Jupiter asked, "Did you carry out my orders?"

Pete and Bob said they had.

"But we didn't want to," Pete grumbled. "Some kids were flying a kite across the road and they may have seen us go in and out our secret entrances."

"It was probably some of Skinny Norris' gang spying on us," Bob explained. "But you said to do it, so we did."

"Excellent." Jupe seemed pleased. "No organization can function unless orders are obeyed. I have had a very interesting afternoon, about which I will tell you later. Now let us tell Taro about some of our adventures."

Jupe's orders seemed to make less and less sense. However, Pete and Bob obeyed. Taro Togati sat silent, listening to their accounts of various cases they had solved. He was especially intrigued by *The Mystery of the Stuttering Parrot*, for he had a trained parrot at home, he told them.

It got darker and darker outside. Through the overhead skylight they could see the night sky turn a deep black.

Then, and only then, did Jupiter unbutton his jacket. They could see what had made him look so fat.

Jupiter was wearing the Golden Belt of the Ancient Emperors!

The great gold links, the huge emeralds, shone richly as, with relief, he took it off and laid it on the table.

"I've been wearing it all day," he said. "It's quite heavy."

Bob and Pete hurled excited questions at him. Where had he found it? Why was he wearing it? Why hadn't he given it back?

Before Jupiter could answer, the trap door from Tunnel Two heaved up under their feet. A tiny man, grimacing horribly and waving a knife, glared up at them. At the same instant the panel from Red Gate Rover swung open and another little man, also armed, appeared.

Timed to coincide exactly, the main door from Easy Three burst in. Two little men, looking fierce and determined despite their size, pointed sharp knives at the boys.

"Okay, kids, we've come for it!" one of them shrilled. "Hand over the belt!"

No adults could have come through the secret entrances to Headquarters. That is, no normal adults. But these were not full-grown men; they were midgets.

As the four midgets swarmed into the little office, Jupiter moved into action.

"Red Alert! Top emergency! Exit instant!" he shouted. He grabbed the Golden Belt and was on top of the desk even as he spoke. He thrust up the skylight, and from outside pulled down a rope with two loops in it for footholds. Taro went up it like a monkey, and Jupe passed him the belt. Pete and Bob, slightly dazed, reacted to automatic training and clambered after him. By the time the angry midgets filled the little office, Jupiter had joined the others on the roof.

It seemed they were trapped there. The midgets, acrobats themselves, were already swarming after them. They shouted exultantly, for there seemed no way for the boys to get down. But Jupiter had provided for just such an emergency.

An old slide from a school play yard stood against the side of the trailer. Beams of steel seemed to block it.

But one by one the boys flung themselves onto the slide and, flat on their stomachs, plummeted onto the sawdust-covered ground below. They dodged around piles of junk, heading for the exit gate.

On the roof of Headquarters, the first midget tried to follow them down the slide. However, he went down sitting, instead of flat, and was brought up with a jolt against a jagged steel beam. His squeal of outrage pierced the night.

"Go back!" he yelled. "Inside and out that way! We've got to catch them!"

There was a scramble on the roof and the midgets swiftly lowered themselves into the office and out through Easy Three.

"We have to find them!" one screeched in a high voice. "They've still got the belt."

The boys, who were hiding in the dark space behind a

pile of lumber, felt a shiver of fear as four tiny shadows, long knives glittering in their hands, came toward them.

Then Bob and Pete received their second surprise of the night. Somewhere a whistle blew loudly. An instant later, half a dozen large figures raced through the main gate and threw themselves on the midgets. The little men twisted and squealed, but they were no match for the policemen and Mr. Saito Togati, who had been waiting outside.

There was a brief, ferocious struggle, and then the midgets were being tightly bound and carried off to a waiting police car. Bob, Pete, Jupiter and Taro crawled out of their hiding place. Little Taro was almost beside himself with joy.

"You see, Father!" he cried. "Plan of Jupiter-san work with brilliance. Belt is recovered and little criminals are caught, also."

"Ah, so!" Mr. Togati said. "Truly, from small books may come large words of advice. Jupiter-san, my humble apologies for rudeness in beginning."

"That's all right, sir," Jupiter said, almost stuttering because he was so pleased with the way things had worked out. "Naturally, you figured the police could do a better job."

"With usual criminals, yes," Mr. Togati agreed. "But not with very unusual criminals such as these. My son, I am pleased with you that you persuaded me to listen to these American friends of yours."

Little Taro almost burst with pleasure at his father's praise.

"Now I take good care of belt." Mr. Togati reverently

touched the golden links. "It is worth much money. You boys save my honor. I shall not forget. Again many thanks. Come, Taro. We must go. But in our memories we remain with you."

Mr. Togati and his son bowed low and then left, taking the Golden Belt with them. Chief of Police Reynolds stayed a few minutes more, asking Jupiter questions.

Bob and Pete stood open-mouthed, trying to figure out what it had all been about. Jupiter's mysterious actions—his sudden revelation that he had the Golden Belt, the invasion of Headquarters by armed midgets, their flight, the appearance of Chief Reynolds and Detective Togati—it was more than Bob and Pete could grasp at once. But Bob finally got the correct idea.

"Jupe!" he said, when the police chief had finally gone, "those midgets who came here after the Golden Belt! Why, I'll bet they were the same ones who helped Mr. Rawley rob the bank, weren't they?"

"Yes, they were," Jupiter agreed. "They're really very complete criminals, and it's time they were caught. They've been getting away with too many crimes disguised as children."

"But—" It was coming to Pete now. "But—hey, wait a minute! Are they also the gang who took the Golden Belt in the first place?"

"They certainly are. I said at the time it had to be the crime of a gang of well-organized men. The midgets are men all right—they're just *little* men. They were disguised as Cub Scouts, of course, which is why they never were suspected. Who'd have thought of child criminals? I might have guessed sooner if Bob had mentioned the gold tooth. But as it is I was able to recover the Golden Belt and the midgets were captured, so no harm is done."

There was still a lot Pete and Bob didn't understand, but they had no doubt Jupiter would explain everything in his own good time. Right at the moment Jupe was looking slightly smug, as he sometimes did when things had worked out the way he planned.

Certainly he had every reason to be pleased. Once again Jupiter Jones had demonstrated his right to be First Investigator!

Chapter Eighteen

Mr. Hitchcock Demands Some Answers

Mr. Alfred Hitchcock, the motion picture director, sat back in his swivel chair. Facing him across his desk in his luxurious Hollywood office sat Pete, Bob and Jupiter. Each of them was scrubbed to shining pinkness and wore his best slacks and shirt.

In his hand Mr. Hitchcock held the bundle of papers which told the story of the riddle of the Golden Belt, and the story of Miss Agawam's gnomes, as Bob had written them up. The boys waited anxiously for Mr. Hitchcock's reaction to the stories.

"Well done, lads," Mr. Hitchcock rumbled at last. "Well done indeed. So you rid my friend Agatha of her gnomes, I see. Of course, in doing so you had to solve a bank robbery, recover the loot, find a missing golden belt of fabulous worth and bring the thieves into the hands of the police. But these are mere trifles. I expect something like that to happen when The Three Investigators get started on a case, no matter how trivial it may seem on the surface."

Bob grinned. So did Pete. Jupiter looked pink with pleasure.

"So dear Agatha's gnomes were midgets in disguise,"

Mr. Hitchcock murmured. "The only possible answer, of course. But tell me—how did she feel when she learned that her nephew Roger knew about Rawley's plot to frighten her with fake gnomes?"

"She was very angry at first," Jupiter said. "But of course, Roger didn't know it was part of a criminal plot to rob the bank. He was very ashamed, so Miss Agawam forgave him. In fact, she actually has decided to sell her home and move to a small apartment by the sea. She says that she'll be more comfortable there."

"I am happy to hear it," Mr. Hitchcock answered. "She is a very fine lady. Well, I believe that clears up all the mysteries surrounding the bank robbery. A most ingenious scheme it was—to become night watchman of an abandoned theater in order to dig a tunnel into the vaults of a nearby bank. Perhaps I can work that into a motion picture some time.

"But now—" Mr. Hitchcock tapped the manuscript— "we come to a part which baffles me greatly. I confess I do not understand about the Golden Belt. How it was stolen. Where it was hidden. How you, Jupiter, enticed the criminal midgets into attacking you so the police could seize them. Please give me a full explanation of these mystifying matters."

"Well, sir—" Jupiter took a deep breath, because he had a lot to tell—"I should have seen it all much sooner, just as soon as we discovered that Miss Agawam's gnomes were midgets in disguise. I should have realized that if midgets could look like gnomes, they could also look like children.

"But I was too slow to put two and two together. Until

Bob told me about seeing a Cub Scout with a gold tooth at the museum."

"Ah!" Mr. Hitchcock leaned forward, greatly interested. "The gold tooth. I've been waiting for that. Pray tell me what even a Sherlock Holmes would deduce from a Cub Scout with a gold tooth?"

"Well," Jupiter said, "small boys lose their teeth and grow new, permanent ones. Everyone knows that. Nobody gives a small boy a gold tooth, because it'll just fall out when the tooth behind it comes through."

"Of course!" Understanding spread over the director's face. "Only a grown boy or a man would have a gold tooth. Exactly. So you realized the little Cub Scout was really a full-grown man!"

"A full-grown little man, a midget, wearing a Cub Scout uniform," Jupiter said. "He and his friends, surrounded by dozens of other small Cub Scouts, went totally unsuspected."

"Astounding," Mr. Hitchcock said. "Such ingenuity should be used for better purposes."

"These particular four midgets are acrobats from Central Europe," Jupiter said. "Work for midgets in Hollywood has been scarce lately, and these four decided to pull a robbery. The Nagasami jewel exhibition came to town. It was announced that there would be a Children's Day, with all children in Scout uniforms admitted free. This gave the midgets a terrific opportunity, for they had often dressed up as children. It was a perfect setup for them.

"At almost the same time, Mr. Rawley came looking for some midgets to impersonate gnomes for him, to help him in the bank robbery.

"The midgets made a deal with Mr. Rawley. Mr. Rawley got a woman friend to dress up like a den mother, and take the midgets inside the museum, dressed as Cub Scouts. The woman hired Mr. Frank, the actor, by mail, to create a diversion inside the museum. When all eyes were turned toward him, the four midgets started up the stairs leading to the balcony. No one noticed them there.

"An instant later the lights went out. I'm sure Mr. Rawley did that, in return for the favor the midgets were doing him. He cut off all electricity and drove away. The midgets were now on the balcony. Meanwhile, down below, children were running around like crazy and everything was in confusion."

"I'll buy that!" Pete chimed in.

"The midgets," Jupiter continued, "had a short piece of nylon rope which the woman with them probably had worn around her waist, under her blouse. Three midgets held the rope, while one climbed down it, kicked in the glass case, grabbed the Golden Belt, and was pulled back up to the balcony."

Mr. Hitchcock looked thoughtful.

"Mmm, yes," he said. "They could manage such a feat, being acrobats, in about thirty seconds. Now I understand why they stole the Golden Belt rather than the Rainbow Jewels. The case holding the Rainbow Jewels was out in the middle of the room, beyond their reach. They took what they could get. No doubt they intended to sell the belt back to the Nagasami Jewelry Company for a very large sum."

"They won't talk," Jupiter told him. "But that's what

Mr. Togati, the detective, thinks. Well, after they stole the belt, they knew they had to hide it because they couldn't carry it out without being seen. So they hid it, very quickly, then hurried downstairs to the main floor in the darkness. Then, in the tremendous confusion, they all left. No one suspected their disguise, and of course they couldn't be caught with the belt because they didn't have it."

"Mmm!" Mr. Hitchcock said. "You say they hid the belt in the museum. Yet, following your suggestion, the museum was thoroughly searched, even the spaces behind the pictures. The belt was not found. Why was it not found?"

"Because the detectives and the guards looked everyplace but the right place," Jupiter said. "The midgets had figured out that hiding place very carefully. They were sure the belt wouldn't be found and they could go back some other time to get it. Actually, they were busy with the bank robbery, so they planned to go on the next Children's Day, when no one would notice them in their Cub Scout uniforms."

"Precisely," Mr. Hitchcock agreed.

"The police hadn't been able to arrest them for the bank robbery. Their friends gave them alibis. It occurred to me that if I could get them to attack me and have the police waiting when they did it, they would be caught red-handed for that crime."

"You could at least have told us what you were up to!" Bob said at this point. "Pete and I were scared stiff when those midgets broke into Headquarters, waving knives at us!"

"Our emergency exit worked perfectly, as I was sure it would," Jupiter told him. "So all was well. You see, Mr. Hitchcock, I hurried to the museum and found Taro Togati, the son of the Japanese detective in charge of guarding the exhibit. He and I and his father found the belt, and I put it on under my jacket——"

"But where did you find it?" Pete couldn't help interrupting.

"I'm coming to that," Jupiter told him. "Anyway, I put the belt on under my jacket and then went to the boarding house where the midgets lived. I seemed to be alone but of course I was followed by plain clothesmen because the Golden Belt is worth probably a million dollars.

"I talked to the midget with the gold tooth, as I knew he had to be one of the gang. He pretended not to know what I was talking about, but he knew perfectly well I had helped break up Rawley's bank robbery.

"I told him I was sorry now I hadn't accepted Rawley's proposition to become a member of the gang. That I wanted to make a lot of money fast. He understood that all right."

"All criminals feel that way," Mr. Hitchcock agreed. "So of course they think everyone else does, too."

"I told him I had the Golden Belt, but didn't know how to get rid of it, and I was willing to sell it for the amount Rawley paid the four of them—forty thousand dollars. I opened my coat and let him see the belt and his eyes almost popped out. He knew it was real, all right, and he knew I must be a crook or I would have reported it to the museum authorities."

Jupiter looked pleased at having been thought a big-time crook.

"I said I'd give him and the others until midnight to think it over. Until then I'd be in my Headquarters in The Jones Salvage Yard with my friends. If they wanted to make a deal, they could come, bringing the money, and we would give them the belt for the money. I knew they wouldn't dare pull anything at the boarding house. There were too many people around."

"Aha!" exclaimed Alfred Hitchcock. "Knowing they were crooks, you felt sure they would try to take the belt from you rather than buy it."

"Yes, sir. But even if they had come to buy it with the money stolen from the bank, that would have been evidence against them."

"So that's why you had us go in and out our secret entrances so much that day!" Bob exclaimed. "Those kids watching us were midgets in disguise. You wanted them to learn all about how to attack us better!"

"Yes, I'll bet they even photographed us from that kite!" Pete said. "Next time you risk our lives, please let us know about it!"

Jupiter Jones squirmed a little in his chair.

"I had perfect faith in Emergency One," he said. "And it was necessary for the midgets to know how to get in. I had Taro with me so that he could win his father's approval. But I couldn't let the midgets know or they would have been suspicious.

"Anyway, I alerted Detective Togati and Chief Reynolds and they were waiting outside, carefully hidden. The midgets attacked us on schedule. We fled, and they were captured. The case was brought to a successful conclusion."

"Indeed it was!" Mr. Hitchcock said. "However—" and he fixed his gaze severely on Jupiter—"you sidestepped my question. So I'll ask it again. Where did the midgets hide the Golden Belt so no one else could find it?"

"Where no one else would look for it," Jupiter said. "I had trouble figuring it out until I remembered they were acrobats. At Miss Agawam's house they stood on each other's shoulders so they could rap on the window. That made me think that maybe in the museum——"

"One moment, young Jupiter!" Mr. Hitchcock boomed. "Light is beginning to dawn for me. Let me see if I can figure out the rest the way you did."

He turned back to the bundle of papers on his desk and leafed through them. He found the one he wanted, read it over again, and nodded.

"Ah, yes," he said. "The clues are all here. On page 18. Everything is clear now."

Bob and Pete tried hard to remember what was on the page he had mentioned. Something about the inside of the museum and the way the pictures were hung. That was all they could remember.

"Yes, indeed," Mr. Hitchcock went on. "In the narrative, it is made clear that a broad molding runs around the wall just under the ceiling of the two rooms with domed ceilings. Such moldings were once used to hang pictures. Also, in large, older houses, moldings were put up as a decoration, to keep the walls from seeming too high.

"Such a molding, large enough, could have a deep

crevice in it, or possibly a flat place on top. Now as I imagine it, the midgets noticed this molding at the museum. They knew no one would ever suspect it as a hiding place. So after they had stolen the belt, they made a human ladder, and the midget on top placed the belt either in the crevice of the molding or along the top, where it could not be spotted from below.

"This took only a moment. An instant later they were ready to flee as four frightened Cub Scouts. Later, no one looked at the molding because it would have taken a ladder to reach it and everyone knew there was no ladder in the room at the time of the robbery. Is that correct, Jupiter?"

Bob and Pete were mentally kicking themselves for not having figured it out for themselves. After all, they had seen the molding. Of course, it was pretty dark up near the ceiling, with no windows.

Jupiter's answer gave them a jolt of surprise.

"No, sir," he told Alfred Hitchcock. "Your answer isn't quite correct, sir."

Mr. Hitchcock's cheeks puffed out. He frowned at Jupiter. His voice deepened.

"Indeed, young man!" he said. "If I had been making a movie of this story, that's the hiding place I'd have chosen. Just where, then, was the belt?"

"I figured it out just as you did, sir," Jupiter said. "But when I got to the museum and climbed up on a ladder, I found the molding was curved. There was no flat place to hold the belt. That stumped me."

"I should think it would," Mr. Hitchcock said.

"Then," Jupiter said, "as I stood there on the ladder

feeling pretty foolish, I felt a current of cool air blowing in my face. That immediately told me the truth——"

"Aha!" Mr. Hitchcock rumbled. "The air conditioning!"

"Yes, sir," Jupiter agreed. "There was an opening just underneath the molding for the special air conditioning installed in the museum. I tried the grillwork on the front, and it came loose. The Golden Belt was hung down inside the air-conditioning duct by a black string. But as you said, the opening was up so high it needed a ladder to reach it, so it hadn't been searched previously."

"Excellent!" Mr. Hitchcock said. "Now everything is clear. You solved two cases, actually, which were connected by the four larcenous midgets involved in both. That was quite an achievement, even for The Three Investigators."

The boys looked at each other and grinned. As they got up to leave, the director asked, "And what is on the agenda now, lads?"

"Skin-diving lessons," replied Pete promptly, and Bob nodded.

Jupiter looked thoughtful. "I wonder," he said, almost to himself, "if further practice in deduction would be more valuable."

Mr. Hitchcock laughed. "Well, whatever you boys take on, I know it will be interesting," he said. "I shall await your next report."

The boys left, and the movie director turned back to Bob's notes on his desk. "Gnomes and a vanishing treasure," he said with a chuckle. "What a movie that would make!"

ALFRED HITCHCOCK
and The Three Investigators Series

The Secret of Terror Castle
The Mystery of the Stuttering Parrot
The Mystery of the Whispering Mummy
The Mystery of the Green Ghost
The Mystery of the Vanishing Treasure
The Secret of Skeleton Island
The Mystery of the Fiery Eye
The Mystery of the Silver Spider
The Mystery of the Screaming Clock
The Mystery of the Moaning Cave
The Mystery of the Talking Skull
The Mystery of the Laughing Shadow
The Secret of the Crooked Cat
The Mystery of the Coughing Dragon
The Mystery of the Flaming Footprints
The Mystery of the Nervous Lion
The Mystery of the Singing Serpent
The Mystery of the Shrinking House
The Secret of Phantom Lake
The Mystery of Monster Mountain
The Secret of the Haunted Mirror
The Mystery of the Dead Man's Riddle
The Mystery of the Invisible Dog
The Mystery of Death Trap Mine
The Mystery of the Dancing Devil
The Mystery of the Headless Horse
The Mystery of the Magic Circle
The Mystery of the Deadly Double
The Mystery of the Sinister Scarecrow
The Secret of Shark Reef